Demon Hunter Ashlyn: Sexy Demon Hunter

Riley Rose

The Sexy Demon Hunter Series

A Story in the Decadent Fantasy Universe

Copyright © 2020 Riley Rose

Cover Design by Sarah of ForCoverService on Fiverr

All rights reserved. No part of this publication may be reproduced, distributed, or transmitted in any form or by any means without the the prior written permission of the author, except in the case of brief quotations for review purposes.

This is a work of fiction and any resemblance to real people, places, or situations is coincidental.

Visit RileyRoseErotica.com for more sexy stories!

CHAPTER ONE

Ashlyn Summersnow loved hunting demons. It was her job after all. And what she was doing right now.

She tore through the underbrush, pursuing the vile creature that had just terrorized the neighboring village.

Her 26 year-old Half-Elf ears picked up a rustle. She deftly spun out of the way as a blur of motion swept past her.

The glowing red eyes of a Lavellan peered at her, angry that it didn't get her with its sneak attack. A Lavellan wasn't exactly a demon. Monster. Weird creature. Whatever you wanted to call it. If it was strange and causing trouble, Ashlyn was called in to handle it.

In this case, she was basically fighting a really huge rat. Except more disgusting and way more dangerous. One bite would imbue the recipient with a deadly poison that would result in a very quick and very painful death.

She plucked twin daggers from either side of her hip, matching the creature's movements as it circled her.

The Lavellan charged. She leapt into the air, flipping over it and slashing its back with one of her daggers. The creature howled and spun around quickly. Something bubbled up in its throat and it spewed forth a mucusy green substance. Straight at Ashlyn!

Ashlyn had never seen a Lavellan do this before. Wow, it was so great when nasty creatures mutated and became even more nasty.

She tried to twist out of the way but the gross slime got over her form-fitting tunic.

"Ahhh!" she yelped in pain, realizing it was some kind of acid.

Acid that was burning through her clothes and about to get on her skin. She tore off all the clothing she was wearing on her torso, revealing her tanned body and firm tits. She wasn't as fair as most Elves. She took more after her human mother in her complexion. She also had her mom to thank for her sensual curves and breasts that were larger than most of her kind. Not huge by any means but they were perfectly shaped and gave her partners in the bedroom plenty to work with. She felt her nipples get erect from the coolness in the forest.

She had just thrown her clothes to the ground when the rat spit another blast of acid, this time onto her leggings. They disintegrated rapidly allowing some of the slime to get on her underwear. She ripped everything off and managed to avoid almost all the acid, though a little singed her upper thigh. That was going to leave a scar.

She stood there completely naked, staring at the Lavellan. What was it with demons and monsters that they always tried to get attractive women naked? Ashlyn wasn't trying to brag. But she had gotten the best of both worlds from her parents. Her auburn hair reached a few inches past her shoulders and framed her exquisite Half-Elf face. She had an athletic, sexy build and her ass was to die for. At least according to the men and maidens she had slept with.

Well, she hoped this super-gross rat was enjoying the view. It was the last thing it was going to see.

She was ready for its acid-spit this time. She snatched her daggers off the ground and used her elf reflexes to dance around the green globs flying at her.

She got close enough to slash across the creature's nose and leg. It screeched and pursued her at full speed.

Ashlyn sprinted straight for a large oak. She ran up it, propelled herself off, and did a backflip above the surprised monster.

She landed on top of it, plunging both daggers down deep. It uttered one last gasp and then lay still.

She stayed there for a moment, catching her breath. *Okay, that could have gone worse.* The only downside was she had to show her tits and ass to a gross rat. But it's not like it was the fist demon or monster to see her naked.

She wiped her daggers off with the remnants of her clothing, then strapped them to her naked thighs.

She glanced back at the forest entrance. Now she just needed to figure out how to get some clothes without a bunch of people gawking at her completely nude body.

*****

Ashlyn crept up to the nearest farm. Clothing and sheets hung on lines outside the house. The wardrobe was plain and basic, and the only things that had a chance of fitting her were dresses. Ashlyn virtually never wore dresses, so she wasn't too excited at the idea of putting one on, but it was better than being naked.

She was examining a particularly ugly frock when she realized she wasn't alone. She looked to the side and saw a boy about 13 years-old staring at her. Well, more like ogling her.

Ashlyn wasn't sure what to do.

"Um, hi." She waved at him. *Yup, great Ashlyn, just keep*

standing here waving as he gawks at your naked tits.

"Mom!" he yelled. "There's a naked elf lady out here stealing our clothes. And she's got great boobs!"

Thanks a lot kid. Ashlyn was about to tell him to shut it when a sturdy woman burst out of the house, wielding a crossbow. Shit, the farmers around here didn't mess around.

Momma Crossbow let loose a bolt. Ashlyn twisted acrobatically as it tore through the sheet in front of her and just barely missed her.

She grabbed an empty water bucket and hurled it at the woman. It struck her in the chest, knocking the crossbow out of her hands and her ass into the pig trough behind her. Her son thought that was very amusing.

Ashlyn knew that was her cue to leave. She hurdled the wooden fence surrounding the house and bolted away from the farm, hearing splashing, cursing, and the woman admonishing her son to "Stop staring at her ass!" Well, at least that kid got the thrill of his life. She, however, was still naked.

*****

After her first farm fiasco, she wasn't taking any chances. She found another farm not too far away and spied on it from behind a nearby grove. She saw a lone man working next to the house. She waited a while, watching. No one else appeared to be home.

She padded up behind him, very self-conscious as she didn't usually do stealth operations in the buff.

She had an arm twisted behind him and a dagger to his throat before he could blink.

"I'm not going to hurt you," she said as nicely as anyone could when holding a dagger to someone's throat. "I just need some clothes."

As she pressed against him, she could feel how muscular he was. Her nipples hardened. *C'mon, Ashlyn, really?*

"O... okay," he stammered. "But why are you naked?"

Of course he knew she was naked. Her stupid projectile tits were jabbing into his back.

"This gross monster melted my clothes off and..." She stopped, realizing how ridiculous it sounded. "Never mind, let's just go in the house and get some clothes."

"Of... of course. You won't need the knife. I'm very happy to help a lady in distress."

She pushed him forward but kept the dagger ready. "I'm not some helpless maiden in distress. I'm a demon hunter."

"You are?" he exclaimed. "Oh wow, I've always wanted to meet..."

He trailed off as he turned around and got a look at her. His mouth hung open.

Oh boy. Here we go.

She put her hands on her hips. "Would you stop gawking at me?"

He turned red and tried to not stare at her. "I... I'm sorry. It's just... I've never seen a more beautiful woman in my life."

Ashlyn's face softened as she studied his. She prided herself on being able to read people. He seemed genuine. Like a nice country lad. While she was scrutinizing his face, she realized how handsome he was. His caramel skin glistening with sweat from his exertions on the farm. His shirt was partly open in the front, his shirtsleeves rolled up. Which gave her a much better view of his rippling muscles.

"Oh, well, that's sweet, I guess," she said awkwardly.

He smiled at her. And actually gazed fully into her eyes and not anywhere lower. Okay that sealed it. He was super-nice. She was totally going to have sex with him.

"Is there anyone else here?"

"No, it's just me."

She sheathed her dagger and took his hand. "Okay, come with me."

She yanked him into the house.

*****

Ashlyn lowered herself onto his extremely impressive cock, moaning in delight as she sunk all the way to its base.

"Oh gods, that feels good," she purred.

She squirmed on top of him, loving how it felt to have his entire shaft inside her.

He shuddered underneath her. "Ohh, by Zirena, you're so tight."

She rubbed her hands along his powerful chest, feeling every muscle. He grabbed her tits and massaged them gently, using his thumbs to play with her nipples. She moaned in pleasure.

She lifted her hips up and forced them back down onto his cock, causing them both to gasp. She rode him slowly as he worked more of his magic on her tits. She was so glad the Lavellan made her get naked. Otherwise, she never would have stopped here and had this amazing cock inside her.

She rode him harder. The bed creaked and shook as its sounds mixed with their increasingly audible moans and sighs. Gods, it felt so good.

He pinched both her nipples, sending shockwaves of pleasure from her tits down her stomach to her already pleasure-ridden pussy. She went even faster. She wanted to take his massive cock as hard as she could. She could feel the orgasm building up in her. She wanted it so badly. She wanted him to shoot his pure farmboy cum in her.

She knew they were both getting close to the fireworks

when they heard the door in the outer room slam open.

"Oh shit! It's my Mom."

"Your Mom?!"

He tossed her off him.

"Ahh!" She fell off the bed and landed on the floor.

She groaned but then went quiet as the door to his room was flung open.

"Corvan, what are you doing in bed when there's work to be done?" she heard a strong female voice ask.

"Oh, I… I wasn't feeling well so I decided to lay down."

"Completely naked?"

"I… ah… was really hot. I think I have a fever."

Ashlyn rolled her eyes in her hiding place. He was a terrible liar.

"Does your fever have anything to do with the naked women hiding behind your bed?"

Oh shit. Ashlyn popped her head up. "Um, hi." *Ugh, why is that the only thing I can say today when I'm in these awkward situations?*

His mom gave her a look only a mother is capable of. Ashlyn wished she was fighting a demon right now.

*****

Ashlyn sat at the meal table, wrapped in a sheet. Corvan sat beside her, his clothes back on. His mom sat across from them, giving them a withering glare that would melt candles.

"So this is what you do when I go to market every day?"

"No, this is the first time I swear!"

Ashlyn gaped at him. *Oh no. I took his virginity.* Shit. That wasn't what she had planned. At most he was only a few years younger than her. She figured he'd had his share of bosomy farmgirls.

"You're a virgin?"

"No, I..." He paused as his mom raised an eyebrow at him. "No, I'm not. I meant it was the first time doing it when I was supposed to be working."

Whew. Ashlyn felt better. But not much as his mom turned her attention from Corvan to her.

"And you, young lady, where are your clothes?"

Ashlyn froze. Usually she was super-confident, especially battling the forces of evil. But under his mom's gaze, she felt like a teenager getting caught having sex for the first time.

She thought about trying to concoct some elaborate story. But the way his mom was looking at her, she knew she better just tell the truth.

"Okay, so I'm a demon hunter. And there was this Lavellan - oh that's a big, gross rat - terrorizing the area, so I hunted it down. But it was a weird mutated one and it spewed out this disgusting acid stuff and it got all other my clothes and burned them so I had to take them off, and then I was fighting the thing in the nude and I killed it but I had no clothes. And I went to your neighbor's farm where this teenage kid loved staring at my boobs and his mom tried to shoot me in the ass with a crossbow and then I came here and was kind of bossy to your son but he was incredibly kind and sweet and looked so hot, so I dragged him into bed and we were having amazing sex when you showed up."

She took a deep breath as she finally finished blurting everything out. Corvan was looking at her dumbfounded. His mom's eyes bore into her. Ashlyn felt like she was about to be scolded like her father would do when she didn't pronounce her Elvish perfectly.

"Um, if you're about to grab a crossbow, could I get a head start first?"

Corvan's mom looked at him. "You see honey. This is the

kind of woman you should be with."

Ashlyn blinked. Um, what?

His mom patted her hand warmly. "And don't worry about the crossbow dear. Our neighbor is a little crazy. She thinks everyone is a thief or bandit or some shapeshifting demon. She tries to shoot anyone she doesn't know."

"Oh," Ashlyn replied, surprised his mom was taking things so well. "You're not mad we were…"

"Shaking the sheets? Tempting the gods? Playing nug-a-nug?"

"Mom!"

Ashlyn didn't even know what nug-a-nug was, but she did know this was the weirdest experience of meeting someone's mom ever.

"Relax honey. I know you've had sex before. We all do it. I mean when your father was alive, he could really…"

"Mom!!"

"To answer your question dear, no I'm not mad. You're not only an extraordinarily beautiful woman but an extremely capable one. You did the whole town a huge service by taking care of that terrible beast. You're the type of woman I hope Corvan falls in love with someday. And I'm sure you can teach him a thing or two in the bedroom."

She put a finger to Corvan's lips before he could protest again.

"Oh, um, okay." Ashlyn was so thrown off by this woman's forthrightness she really didn't know what to say. But she did know she was really starting to like her. Besides the super-nice things she said about her, Ashlyn liked that she said whatever was on her mind and didn't hold back. It was refreshing.

"Oh where are my manners? I don't even know your name. If you're going to be banging my son, it's only proper to introduce ourselves."

Corvan dropped his forehead against the table. Ashlyn would have laughed, but she was too busy turning red.

"I'm Rima," his mom said, taking Ashlyn's hand in both of hers and rubbing it in a very motherly way. Ashlyn could feel the same strength Corvan had in his hands, and also the same tenderness.

"I'm... Ashlyn."

"What a lovely name."

"Almost as lovely as the woman it belongs to," Corvan declared, gazing into Ashlyn's eyes.

Ashlyn had to admit, it was a really good line. And she could tell it wasn't one just to get her in bed. She already proved she was happy to do that with him. He was really sincere.

"Oh no," Rima sighed. "I forgot to get something at the market."

Ashlyn smiled. She was just as bad a liar as her son.

"I better go right now. And I'm sure I'll get to talking to Mr. Vadrisci. You know how he goes on. I'll probably be gone quite a while."

She patted Ashlyn's hand again. "So dear, please have as much sex with my son as you want. I'll see what I can do about finding you some clothes."

"Oh, um... thank you."

"Oh no need to thank me dear. It's not just for you. If the lads and lassies around here got a look at you in the buff, they'd all leave town to go find themselves a Half-Elf as lovely as you to court."

Ashlyn blushed. She couldn't remember the last time she felt this embarrassed and awkward. But oddly she didn't mind. She felt a warmness being around Rima and Corvan.

Rima rose from the table. "Okay I'm off. Just don't get married until I get back."

"Mom!"

"I'm just teasing honey." She kissed him on the head. Then scooted around the table and kissed Ashlyn on the cheek. Ashlyn was surprised but didn't mind. It was rather nice actually.

The door slammed shut and they heard her singing a jaunty tune as she headed into town.

Corvan scratched his head. "So… that's my mom."

"I like her. A lot."

"Really? Thank the gods. I thought she would have scared you away for sure."

Ashlyn laughed. "Not at all. I can see where you get your kindness from."

He looked down, blushing a little.

She punched him.

"Ow! What was that for?"

"For tossing me onto the floor you nitwit."

"Oh right. I'm really sorry. I panicked."

"Mmm, guess I'm not taking you demon hunting."

"But can you tell me all about it? I want to hear everything."

"Yes, but first you need to bend me over this table and finish giving me the fucking of my life."

He didn't need to be asked twice.

He pulled her to her feet and yanked the sheet off her, making her spin around as it unraveled. He caught her mid-spin and used her momentum to swirl her onto the table, her tits pressed against the linen tablecloth.

Before she could get her bearings from whirling around, he was deep inside her. *Holy shit!* She loved his fucking cock so much. He clasped her hips firmly, his gentle fingers kneading her smooth skin, and began to give her the fucking she craved.

"By the goddess!" The way he was filling her was driving

her wild. She writhed on the table as he plunged every ounce of her. His own groans joined her sultry symphony.

She thrust her hands toward him, hoping he would grab them. He seized her wrists and pulled her back into him, making her take every possible inch of his throbbing cock.

Her head and tits were lifted off the table as he kept yanking her ferociously onto his shaft. Any sound that left her mouth was completely incomprehensible. She really needed to fuck farmboys more often.

Her orgasm hit her like a freight train. She yelled/moaned/shrieked in ecstasy as her juices came pouring out of her. He released her hands and let her drop to the table, watching her squirm on the table, her orgasms making her spasm uncontrollably.

As she began to recover, he withdrew his still fully erect sword and lifted her off the table. He spun her to face him and lowered her onto his pulsating cock.

Goddess preserve me! She wrapped her legs around his waist, her arms around his neck. And clung to him tightly as she felt how deeply she was speared with his cock.

He grabbed her waist and raised her up, just keeping the head inside her. Then forced her down to his hilt.

"Uhhhhh," she groaned, not believing how good it felt.

She let him use her body to fuck his enormous cock. He was so strong he had no problem doing it. And she had no problem letting him use her as a sex toy. She was kick-ass and take charge in battle. But when it came to kinkier stuff, she loved giving herself over to her partners and letting them have their way with her.

His large hands moved to her hips, his fingers squeezing her ass. This allowed him to force her onto him even deeper and harder. *Ohhhh!* She loved the feeling of his powerful hands on her ass. It made her want his cock even more.

She kissed him as he continued to make her take everything he had. Her tongue found his. It tasted sweet and salty, like her favorite candy. She panted and moaned into his mouth as he shoved her pussy down onto him with more intensity.

"Fuck, I... I'm going to cum again!" she cried as his cock rammed up into her.

"Me... me too!" he grunted.

He thrust her hips as fast as he could onto him. Their screams were so loud, his crossbow-wielding neighbor and her horny son probably heard them.

Ashlyn felt him seize up inside her. Felt his cock expand momentarily. And then felt a huge force of his cum shoot up into her. Her own orgasm followed just after. As his juices were flowing up into her, hers were flowing down his cock and onto the floor. She made a mental note to make sure they cleaned everything up so his mom didn't kill them.

They clung to each other as their bodies spasmed from their ongoing orgasms. Her arms and thighs clutched his back and hips, never wanting to be apart from his body. His fingers dug into her ass more powerfully than anyone had ever held her.

They slowly eased their passionate grips as their orgasms subsided, though she shuddered as he shot a few more spurts into her. He eased her off his cock and let her get her feet back underneath her. She placed her arms against his powerful chest and lay against him. He held her tight, running his hands down her toned back until he reached her ass. He squeezed it gently.

She purred in his arms. "That was amazing."

"Mmm, I think my mom was right. I'm going to be obsessed with Half-Elves after this."

She gazed into his sweet chocolate eyes and kissed him. She took his hand. "C'mon."

"Where are we going?"

"To have a lot more sex obviously."

And that they did.

He fucked her against the side of the barn.

She rode him inside the barn on a pile of hay.

They had sex underwater in the small lake near his farm.

They fucked in the woods on the way back from the lake, trying not to get pine cones up their asses.

And finally, they did it in the fields outside his house, the long grass tickling their naked bodies. They went more slowly and gently this time. Having worn themselves out from their previous exertions. And at this point, knowing each other's bodies so well, it just felt comfortable having him inside her.

"Gods above! Are you two still going at it?"

They sat up like a shot. And saw Rima holding sacks of food and staring at them.

Ashlyn scurried behind Corvan, using his body to attempt to cover her nudity and her reddening face. Corvan snatched a leaf and put it in front of his crotch, though quite frankly it wasn't big enough since he was still hard from being inside Ashlyn.

"Would you two stop being so foolish? Corvan, it's not like I haven't seen your winky a million times."

Ashlyn grinned and whispered in his ear. "I really like your winky."

"Well, that's obvious since you were grinding corn with my son for the past three hours."

Ashlyn thought she had good hearing as a Half-Elf. This woman was putting her to shame. She was also making her turn every shade of red imaginable.

"And stop covering up dear. With the tits and ass you have, you should want to show them off to everyone."

"Oh gods," Corvan groaned and fell over, hiding in the grass, which he apparently thought would save him from further embarrassment.

It also meant Ashlyn's assets were on full display for Rima.

She waved meekly at the no-nonsense woman. "Um, can I help you with the food?"

"Thank you dear. That's lovely of you to offer. Get your hot Half-Elf tits and ass over here and take this satchel."

Ashlyn hurried over to her. She was not going to disobey this woman. And somehow Rima made "Half-Elf tits and ass" actually sound like a term of endearment. If Ashlyn didn't love her own mother so much, she would have probably asked Rima to adopt her.

She took one of the bags from Rima and headed toward the house with her.

"Corvan, stop playing around in the grass. You think the women should do all the work around here?"

"Yes ma'am." He hopped up, holding more leaves over his crotch as he scuttled after them.

*****

Ashlyn stood next to Rima, helping her chop carrots on the wooden counter. Corvan had just finished setting the table and was now sweeping the floor behind them. Ashlyn noticed out of the corner of her eye he was also surreptitiously cleaning up their love making juices.

"That outfit looks so cute on you," Rima remarked.

Ashlyn looked down at her clothes. Rima had been very thoughtful and bought clothes for Ashlyn at the market. Corvan was so much larger than Ashlyn and Rima so much shorter that neither of their clothes would have fit her. Rima had found something the perfect size for her.

It was a forest green tunic that tied around the waist and stretched to Ashlyn's upper thighs, complementing her reddish-brown hair nicely. Form-fitting emerald leggings matched her eyes. They weren't as durable as her normal leggings. These were more to show off Ashlyn's curves, but she had to admit they were super-comfortable. Ankle-high leather boots completed the ensemble.

Ashlyn usually picked clothing that would be good for hunting and fighting, so this was a little different for her. But Rima was right. She did look pretty adorable in them. And Corvan apparently thought so too, as he kept stealing glances at her. And he had seen her naked this entire time, so that was saying something.

"Thank you," she told Rima. "I'll pay you back for it."

"You certainly will not. It's my gift to you. It's the least I can do for the gift you gave me."

"But.. I didn't give you anything."

"Yes you did. You brought my son happiness. Why do you think he keeps glancing at you with that goofy grin on his face?"

Ashlyn glanced over her shoulder and smiled. He was giving her one of those goofy grins right now.

Rima watched them for a moment. "All right you two, help me bring the food to the table."

After setting out the plain but hearty feast, Rima said a quick prayer to Pherena, Goddess of the Dawn. That was the main human goddess Ashlyn grew up learning about, so she could appreciate the prayer. Elven gods were a whole other matter. Being half-human and half-elf meant learning a lot about two totally different cultures.

They dug in to the filling meat, potatoes, and vegetables. Ashlyn ate voraciously. All that monster hunting and sex marathoning had made her famished.

Corvan looked at her with a grin.

"What?" she asked, her mouth full. "Do I have food on my

face?" That was something she had a tendency to do, so it was quite likely.

"Ashlyn don't talk with your mouth full," Rima scolded.

Ashlyn swallowed the potatoes, looking chagrined. "Sorry."

Corvan chuckled. "No your face looks lovely. I was just thinking how ridiculous it was that when you first snuck up behind me today, I thought you might have been the succubus people have been talking about."

Ashlyn dropped the roll she was about to chomp into. "Succubus?"

"Corvan stop spreading those ridiculous rumors. There's no succubus. Just a lot of horny people who can't keep it in their trousers."

Ashlyn had gone up against succubi before. She had managed to defeat them, but just barely. They were formidable creatures and not to be taken lightly.

"Why do people think there's a succubus here?"

"Well, multiple people have had dreams they swore were more real than any they've had before. Where the most beautiful woman they've ever seen visits them and does unimaginable pleasurable things to them. And then they wake up exhausted the next morning."

"Of course they're exhausted," piped in Rima. "They're a bunch of drunks or layabouts."

"Mom, some of them, like Kade and Anais, are hard-working, honest folk."

"Well, they probably just got worked up by all the others' rumormongering.

"Has anyone died?" Ashlyn interrupted.

"No," Corvan told her. "They just say they're really tired. Like they don't have much energy."

"How many times have they supposedly been visited?"

"Just once or twice."

Hmm. That was unusual. Once a succubus latched onto her prey, she kept coming back until she sucked every last bit of sexual energy out of them, which usually resulted in the person dying.

"And these people have recovered?"

"Yes they're all fine," Rima answered. "That's why I think it's all a bunch of hogwash. But you're the expert at demon hunting dear. Oh and apparently at fucking my son."

Ashlyn and Corvan both spit out their water at the same time.

"Mom!"

"Rima!"

Rima giggled. "I'm sorry. I shouldn't tease you two so much, but I just can't help it. You're so adorable together."

"Would you like to go for a walk?" Corvan invited Ashlyn.

Ashlyn looked at all the plates on the table.

"Go, go!" Rima said, reading her mind. "I'll clean up here. You two go have fun."

Corvan kissed Rima on the cheek. "Thanks Mom."

"The food was delicious," Ashlyn told her.

She hesitated. Then rushed up to Rima and kissed her on the cheek, scurrying away just as quickly.

Corvan took Ashlyn's hand and led her out of the house.

Rima beamed as she watched them go.

*****

Ashlyn and Corvan walked hand-in-hand through the thick grass and crisp night air. The stars shone brightly above them, and nocturnal critters made faint noises from the forest.

He held her hand tightly but softly. She liked how it felt. She sighed. If her crazy demon hunting didn't take her across the five lands, she could see herself totally falling for him.

"What's wrong?" he asked gently.

She gazed into his deep, chestnut eyes. "Nothing, it's just… I…"

"Can't stay here."

"Yeah."

"It's okay."

"I wish…"

"I know."

He put his arm around her shoulder. She slipped hers across his waist. They held each other close as they walked in silence.

They reached the top of a small hill. They could see smoke coming from the hearths of the scattered farms and the tiny hint of torchlight from the town off in the distance.

"When you're back this way, will you come visit?"

"Yes. Absolutely." She grinned. "If only to see your mom embarrass you more."

He returned the smile. "Is that the only reason?"

She wrapped her arms around his neck. "No. Definitely not the only reason."

He enveloped her waist and pulled her into one of the most amazing kisses she had ever experienced. Their lips and tongues flowed like water. Tasted as sweet as honey. And felt like fireflies giving off sparks of energy.

She rubbed the back of his neck as his fingers ran through her hair. It felt so good to be in his arms. In his lips. Pressed against the tautness of his body.

Their lips parted for a moment. She could feel his breath warm against her face.

"Can I… touch your ears?"

She smiled. "I'd really like that." As a Half-Elf, her ears were super-sensitive to touch. They were way more of an erogenous zone on her than on humans. She loved when her ears were touched, kissed, licked, nibbled, whatever. She kissed him again, thinking about how sweet it was that he asked her first.

As they continued to kiss, his hand found her left ear, his thumb tracing the inside curves of it. She shuddered against him.

He ran his finger and thumb all along the ear up to its pointed end, squeezing it gently. She gasped into his mouth.

"Is that okay?"

"More than okay."

She pulled his head forward to her ear. His tongue darted out and explored all its crevices. She squealed in delight and dug her fingers into the back of his neck.

She squirmed against his rock-hard body as his tongue and mouth did the most amazing things to her ears. She would have fallen to her knees if he wasn't holding her around her waist so firmly.

He eased her down to the soft grass, laying her on her back and straddling her with his knees. He removed his shirt and she ran her fingers along his chest.

He untied her tunic and lifted it over her head, her nipples immediately hardening from the slight chill in the air. He took off her boots and pulled down her leggings, revealing her in all her bare glory.

He took a minute to admire her. She put her arms over her head and let them fall on the grass, not minding one bit that he was taking in all her curves.

"You know, since we've known each other, I've probably had clothes on for like all of 20 minutes."

"And the bad part about that is…"

She whacked him with her thigh playfully. He took off his pants, displaying the fully erect cock she had gotten to know so well today.

He lowered himself gently and entered her slowly. She murmured contently as she felt the warmness from his body cover her inside and out.

They kissed softly as their bodies moved as one. Like a ship riding the waves at sea. They didn't go hard or rough. They had expended a lot of energy doing that earlier. But it wasn't just that. They knew this was the last time they'd be together for quite a while, and they both wanted it to be special.

Ashlyn got completely lost. In his eyes. His lips. His body. It felt like they made love forever.

She lay against his chest afterward, the cool grass underneath her dissipated by the warmth of his arms around her.

They stared up at the heavens, seeing what designs they could make out of the stars. It was the most at peace she had felt in a long time.

*****

They walked back to the house. Holding hands again. Not needing to say anything. Just content to be with each other.

As they got closer, they heard Rima yelling obscenities. They crested a hill and saw a group of bandits surrounding the house.

"By Pherena!" Corvan exclaimed.

Ashlyn was off like a bolt of lightning, hurtling down the hill. She could hear Corvan trying to keep up behind her. She cursed silently at having left her daggers in the house. Goddess forbid she try to have a little romance without some slimy monsters or scummy outlaws causing trouble.

But she wasn't too concerned. She didn't need weapons to kick ass.

She spotted the leader of the scumbags. He was pointing his dirty finger in Rima's face. Rima, of course, wasn't backing down. She leveled a cast iron frying pan at him. Gods, Ashlyn loved this woman.

Ashlyn was like the wind, moving through the bandits before they even realized she was there.

Her palm struck upward against the leader's nose, causing a tidal wave of blood to spew out of it. She threw him against the side of the house, rammed her knee into his dick, and then kicked down hard against his kneecap, breaking his leg.

He screeched in pain as he crumpled to the ground.

The other bandits were frozen in shock. Staring in horror at what just happened.

Ashlyn eyed them like a demon or monster she was hunting. Take out the leader and you destroy the morale of the rest.

Corvan came barreling in, smashing into the nearest bandit. The outlaw crashed through a fence and landed face first in the mud of the pig pen.

Ashlyn saw Corvan grab another bandit and then turned her attention to the rest.

She flitted through them. Her hands, elbows, knees, and feet striking expertly. She was a flash of green and red among the dull mud-brown of the bandits' filthy clothing.

One by one they fell. The second to last one lunged at her with his second-rate sword. She leapt over him, spinning upside down and grabbing his arm and shoulder. She landed and used her momentum to flip him, smashing him onto his ugly bandit head. She twirled and finished the last bandit with a spinning kick to the temple.

She glanced behind her. There were two bandits she had missed. Corvan leveled one with a right hook. Ashlyn smiled approvingly. He obviously had no combat training, but he held his own nicely.

One last outlaw was trying to sneak away, but Rima clanged him over the head with her frying pan. He dropped in a heap. Ashlyn grinned. Go Momma Rima!

The smile slipped off her face as her gaze fell on the bandit leader, who was trying to stand on his one good leg. She snatched a dagger off one of the groaning lackeys and was on the leader in an instant.

She grabbed him by the throat with one hand and held the dagger to his balls with the other.

"Listen up you Orc's cock. If you ever bother these people again, I will hunt you down, cut off your dicks, and shove them down your fucking throats. I'm a demon hunter, so hunting you rancid fucks down will be child's play to me. So you're going to take your rantallion band and hobble back to town and turn yourself in to the local constable. And if you haven't when I get there tomorrow, I will bring the wrath of Shadses down on your asses."

The leader looked so petrified she thought he might have just shit himself. But it was hard to tell because he already smelled putrid.

He motioned for his men to leave. They staggered to their feet and helped each other limp toward town.

Ashlyn glared at them and then softened as she turned to Corvan and Rima. They were staring at her, their mouths hanging open. Shit. She forgot how intense she could get. Well, not usually. Just when anyone tried to threaten people she cared about.

She looked at her feet, embarrassed that she used such coarse language in front of Rima.

"Oh, um, I'm really sorry about all the violence and the cursing. You must…"

She didn't have a chance to finish as Rima flung her arms

around her, giving Ashlyn perhaps the tightest hug she had ever received. She could see strong arms ran in the family.

Corvan ran over and made it a group hug. Ashlyn held onto them fondly.

"You are the most amazing woman I have ever met," Corvan told her, flashing a huge smile.

"You can say that again," Rima agreed. "You were like the goddess Nyvna herself. Are you sure you don't want to marry my son? Like right now."

"Mom!"

Ashlyn blushed a little, but she didn't mind. Rima's ribbing made her feel right at home.

"I'm kidding, I'm kidding. Well, not totally kidding, but okay, okay, I'll stop. Here come inside and I'll give you both some dessert."

Ashlyn's eyes lit up. "Oh goddess, I love dessert! What kind?"

Rima started to list off the options as Ashlyn hooked her arm in Corvan's and went inside.

*****

Ashlyn spent the night in Corvan's arms. Curled up against him in his bed. They didn't do anything except sleep, but she felt as comfortable and safe as she had in her entire life.

Rima fed her a ridiculously huge breakfast and packed even more food for her to take with her. She smiled at the woman who had become like her second mom. Then hugged her fiercely.

She gave Corvan just as ferocious a hug. Then kissed him sweetly.

After tears and more hugging, she finally headed out.

She looked back at the top of a hill and saw them waving in

the doorway. She smiled and waved back.

Then headed down the hill and toward the town.

She wiped a tear away, hoping her travels wouldn't keep her from this region for too long.

She adjusted the pack on her back and marched forward.

She had a succubus to hunt.

CHAPTER TWO

Ashlyn crouched in a tree outside the lovely young maiden's window. She watched her undress, her creamy skin glistening in the moonlight.

Her large breasts bounced slightly as she turned and Ashlyn got a wonderful view of her sensual curves.

Ashlyn felt her nipples get hard against her forest green tunic. She felt like a peeping Neeper spying on the woman. But she wasn't doing it to be creepy. She was waiting for a demon.

Corvan and Rima had told her about a succubus terrorizing the nearby town of Rivervale, which is where she was right now. Maybe terrorizing wasn't the right word. Ashlyn supposed giving people the most amazing sexual experiences of their lives wasn't that bad. Except that succubi usually didn't stop until they had drained all the energy out of their victims and left them lifeless.

But this succubus apparently wasn't doing that. She was flitting from sexy townsperson to townsperson, fucking them and taking some of their sexual energy, but not killing them. That was strange. Ashlyn hadn't encountered a succubus before who did that. She was curious to see if it really was the most sexy of demons she was hunting.

She was camped outside the maiden's window because she was the most beautiful woman in town that hadn't already been visited by the sexual creature. Ashlyn figured she was the most likely candidate for a succubus nighttime snack.

It was just a bonus that she was getting to see the young woman in all her naked glory. She knew she should turn away, but hey, she might miss the succubus if she didn't pay rapt attention. Like really rapt attention.

Ashlyn felt her crotch moisten. Shit. She never could resist a pretty small town girl.

She was trying to figure out how to position herself in the tree and touch herself when she saw a shadow flit across the window. The curtains billowed out but there wasn't any breeze.

The succubus.

Ashlyn sprang from her perch and leapt to the window. She just caught the sill and hoisted herself up and through the lavender curtains.

Her breath caught as she took in the scene. The maiden was sprawled on her back on her bed and the most beautiful, sensual creature Ashlyn had ever seen was on top of her.

The creature had dark purple skin, curved horns that just protruded above her long black locks specked with purple. A long, sinuous tail protruded just above the most perfect ass Ashlyn had seen in the five lands. Every curve on the succubus's body was as sensual as possible. Her succulent breasts, hips, and legs curved in ways that made Ashlyn instantly wet between her legs.

The demon was wrapped around the innocent maiden, fingers inside her, lips fastened to her, sucking the sexual energy out of her.

Damn, this succubus worked fast. It only took Ashlyn a few seconds to get inside the house and the succubus was already inside the maiden's creamy folds.

The young lass was in a state of absolute bliss. Completely enraptured by the succubus and crying out in delight.

Ashlyn realized she was just standing there, staring at them. Well, it was probably the most erotic thing she had witnessed that didn't involve her being naked.

She had forgotten just how powerful the allure of a succubus was. As a demon hunter, she had trained herself to be able to resist most demons' powers, at least to some degree. But she still had to be careful. One little slip and she could find herself enthralled with the ridiculously sensual creature before her.

She snapped herself out of her ogling of the two gorgeous women and leapt onto the bed, tackling the succubus off it.

As soon as her body came in contact with the naked flesh of the creature, Ashlyn felt her pulse quicken and her desire immediately increase. Shit. This succubus was more powerful than the other ones she had encountered.

She focused her mind, trying not to think about that luscious purple skin pressed against her taut Half-Elf body, caressing every inch of her.

She rolled onto the floor and kicked the succubus off her and into the wall.

She grabbed a glass of water off the stand next to the bed and hurled the contents at the still writhing woman on the bed.

It splashed across her face, and she woke up from her sexual reverie. To say the maiden was shocked was a bit of an understatement. She glanced down her very naked body, saw the wetness between her legs, and then saw a Half-Elf and succubus in the room with her.

"Get out of here!" Ashlyn ordered before the woman could freak out. "Now!"

She bolted out of the room, not bothering to cover up.

Ashlyn noticed the sexy way her ass jiggled as she left. Dammit, that succubus was making her super-horny.

As she turned her attention across the room, the sexy demon pounced on her and their momentum carried them onto the bed, the succubus pinning Ashlyn on her back.

Ashlyn breathed in her scent. She was lavender and wildberries. She knew a succubus could smell like whatever you found most appealing. That knowledge didn't help her not get hot from having the alluring creature pressed this closely to her. She could feel every perfectly sensual curve of the body laying on top of her. A body she wanted to explore so badly.

"You scared away my snack," the succubus purred melodiously. "But you'll be an even tastier treat."

Ashlyn was kind of flattered the demon thought she was even hotter than the sexy maiden she was enjoying. She also was getting lost in the succubus's vibrant, violet eyes. She was so beautiful. The most beautiful woman she had ever seen.

C'mon Ashlyn. Snap out of it. You're here to dispatch this thing. Not fuck it.

She grabbed the succubus and flipped her over her head. The nimble creature landed on her feet and bounded out the window.

"Catch me if you can, you sexy demon hunter," she called as she dropped out of view.

Why couldn't things ever be easy? Ashlyn rolled off the bed and leapt out the window, catching a branch and swinging to the ground.

She spotted the succubus as she seemed to melt into the darkness. Luckily, Ashlyn's elven heritage gave her superior vision at night, and she was still able to make out the curvy form of the fleeing, flirty creature.

The succubus was fast. But so was Ashlyn. She hurtled food carts and barrels in the deserted nighttime streets, gaining on the sensual demon in front of her.

The succubus darted up an abandoned building on the outskirts of town. Ashlyn leapt onto a windowsill and propelled herself up the outside of the house.

She snatched the creature's tail just before she was able to pull herself into a third story window. She heard a yelp from the demon above her as she tried to free herself.

As Ashlyn yanked on the tail, the moonlight hit the succubus just the right way so Ashlyn had an amazing view of her perfectly formed ass and delicious pussy. A pussy that was getting very wet.

"Oh yes, yank it harder!" the succubus moaned from above.

What the hell? She was getting turned on by the way Ashlyn was feeling up her tail. Shit. Ashlyn forgot the tail was a huge erogenous zone for a succubus.

Well, she wasn't letting her get away, so she was just going to keep jerking her off until she pulled the succulent creature down.

Juices dripped out of the extremely desirable pussy above her and fell onto her face, some of them running into her mouth. Ashlyn was going to turn away, but the demon's cum tasted so sweet and delicious, she found herself wanting more.

She used her hands to stroke the succubus's tail more seductively and drank up the sweet nectar that was pouring out of the tight cavern above her.

"Ohhh, yes, stroke me harder you Half-Elf slut!"

Ashlyn would have taken offense at that except she was too busy slurping up the deliciousness dripping into her mouth.

She knew it was ridiculous that she was on the side of a building whacking off a super-hot succubus and drinking her cum. But gods it tasted so good.

More juices ran down the succubus's tail, and Ashlyn felt her grip begin to slip. She grasped at the sexy tail, but the juices were completely covering it. Stupid succubus and her non-stop sweet cum.

Ashlyn yelled as she lost her grip and plummeted. Her fingertips just barely managed to catch the window below her, and she dangled there by one hand. She spotted the succubus disappear into the house, one last spurt of succulent sauce emanating from her sexy pussy and splattering onto Ashlyn's face.

Ashlyn was now covered pretty well in the delectable sweetness of the succubus. She tried to ignore that and the burning desire between her legs as she got her other hand on the window and sprang upward.

She soared through the third story window and immediately felt a tendril wrap around her ankle. The succubus tripped her with her tail.

Ashlyn did an acrobatic springboard off the floor with her hands and flipped back to her feet, avoiding the rest of the succubus's attack and kneeing the creature in the stomach.

She rolled over the demon and clung to her back, wrapping her legs around her waist and her arms around her neck.

The succubus struggled to free herself as Ashlyn tightened her grip. She rammed Ashlyn back against the nearest wall. The Half-Elf's breath was knocked out of her, and she slipped off the demon's back.

The creature spun around and took Ashlyn's breath away again. But this time by kissing her. It was the most amazing and sensual kiss of Ashlyn's life. She opened her mouth and let her tongue become one with the demon's. It felt like her entire body was melting into the succubus. She felt like she was in paradise and the succubus's lips were heaven itself.

"What's your name sweetness?" the succubus said between breathtaking smooches.

"Ash... Ashlyn," she managed to get out. She didn't know

why she was telling the creature her name. But it seemed like the right thing to do.

"Mmm," the demon purred. "A name as beautiful as the woman it belongs to. I'm Thalia. When I first saw you I knew I had to have you. But now with my cum all over your face, I want you even more."

She licked some of her juices off Ashlyn's cheek, running her tongue over her own lips seductively.

Ashlyn stared at those lips. Those full, succulent lips she needed pressing against hers.

And then she realized what she was doing. She shoved Thalia away as she shook the cobwebs out.

"Stay out of my head demon!"

"I don't want to be in your head. I want to be in your pants," Thalia said with a mischievous grin.

She held up a ripped tunic in her hand. It looked just like Ashlyn's.

"By the way, missing something?"

Ashlyn looked down at her bare chest. Her firm and lively tits heaving and her nipples hard as granite.

It was Ashlyn's tunic. Thalia must have ripped it off when Ashlyn shoved her away, but Ashlyn was so intoxicated with Thalia she didn't even notice.

Dammit. Ashlyn was usually able to resist demons much more effectively. What was it about this sexy succubus that was affecting her so much?

"Hey, give that back! And stop staring at my tits!"

She snatched at the tunic, but the demon played keep away.

"I can't do that. They're way too perfect to keep them covered up. I especially like how you're jiggling them for me."

"I am not jiggling them for…"

Ashlyn stopped as she realized the madder she got the more her breasts were indeed bouncing around provocatively.

Stupid, sexy succubus.

She covered her chest with her arms, not wanting to provide any more titillation to this annoying but incredibly sensual creature.

That gave Thalia the opportunity to tackle her and rip her leggings and panties off. Leaving Ashlyn totally in the buff.

"Would you stop taking my clothes off!"

Ashlyn scrambled to her feet, not even bothering to cover up now that she was completely naked. She had a serious problem keeping her clothes on recently. She also kind of wanted to show off her perky tits and sensual ass to Thalia.

"Well sure, now that I have you completely naked. You are one incredibly sexy Half-Elf. Can we please make love now?"

Ashlyn tried to cover up her reddening cheeks by doing more yelling.

"What? No we can't make love! I'm trying to send your ass back to Shadses."

"Wouldn't you rather do something else to it?"

Thalia placed her hands on the opposite wall, leaned forward and raised her tail, putting her smooth, delectable ass on display. It had the perfect combination of tone and jiggle, and Ashlyn couldn't take her eyes off it.

She did really want to do something else to it. And she wanted Thalia to do all sorts of wicked things to her.

She felt the wetness grow between her thighs. Dammit. Why couldn't she stop thinking about banging Thalia? Well, probably because she was the most beautiful, sexiest creature she had ever seen and she was using her super-succubus charm to lull Ashlyn into a state of extreme sexual desire.

But Ashlyn also knew she could resist it much more if she really wanted to. A big part of her didn't want to. That part wanted to completely give herself over to Thalia.

She managed to just barely control herself as she

remembered something.

"Wait a minute. Why did you ask me if I wanted to make love instead of just trying to take me? And why have you left all your victims alive?"

Thalia stiffened for a moment. Then spun around, a smile on her face that Ashlyn thought was just a little too forced.

"Because I was waiting for someone with a body as amazing and sexual as yours. The others pale in comparison to your loveliness."

She approached Ashlyn slowly, swaying her hips in ways that shouldn't be legal.

Ashlyn didn't move away.

"I bet you say that to all the girls."

Thalia pouted as if hurt by Ashlyn not believing her.

"Okay, fine, I do. But there's something different about you. I really, really want to explore that tight, wet pussy of yours, make your tits dance in ways you never imagined, and treat your ass like the sex toy it is."

Ashlyn blushed furiously. She loved dirty talk, but Thalia had a way to make her feel way dirtier than usual. She was imagining all the things Thalia just described and how her ass should be the succubus's sex toy.

When she came out of her daydream, Thalia was right in front of her, her violet lips inches from Ashlyn's. She could feel the sexy demon's warm breath on her face.

And then she was kissing Thalia. Letting the succubus explore every part of her mouth and twist her tongue in ways that made Ashlyn moan submissively.

She felt Thalia's hands trace down her smooth back and find her ass. Ashlyn gasped into Thalia's mouth as the demon squeezed it the exact perfect amount to make Ashlyn melt into her body and give herself over to the succubus.

"You have the most delicious ass," Thalia told her. "You

like the way I'm playing with it, don't you?"

"Y... yes."

She wrapped her arms around Thalia's neck and let her do things to her ass that made her squirm in delight.

Thalia's tongue tasted like the sweetest fruit Ashlyn could imagine. And she couldn't get enough of it. Thalia's large, perfect tits pressed against Ashlyn's and their nipples rubbed together in delicious harmony.

Ashlyn had never wanted someone so much as she wanted Thalia. She loved the feel of every curve of the demon's body writhing against her.

Thalia moved behind Ashlyn and ran her hands up her stomach until she had both of the Half-Elf's firm tits in her soft hands.

Ashlyn arched back against Thalia, whimpering as the succubus worked her breasts and nipples like a master sculptor working clay.

Thalia moved sensually against her, whispering into her ear.

"Mmm, your body feels so good. We're going to have so much fun together."

Ashlyn shifted her weight.

"We sure are."

And with that, she seized Thalia's arm, twisted her body, and flipped Thalia over her hip.

The succubus crashed hard onto the floor. Ashlyn immediately snatched some rope from her belt pouch lying on the floor and tied Thalia's hands behind her to her ankles.

She knelt in front of the demon, who was also forced to be in a kneeling position, her legs spread apart, her delicious and inviting pussy prominently displayed.

For the first time tonight, Ashlyn saw genuine surprise on the succubus's face.

"What... How..."

Ashlyn smiled. She felt like Thalia had the upperhand up until this point. It was nice to put the sexy succubus in her place.

"I'm a Demon Hunter. And I'm very good at what I do."

She tried to say it like she hadn't been on the verge of being utterly seduced by Thalia. She had so wanted to completely surrender to the beautiful creature, and it had required every ounce of her training and willpower to resist her.

"Is that why you tied me up in such a provocative position, with my wet, tight pussy all ready for you?"

Dammit. Thalia was good. She may have been momentarily surprised by Ashlyn resisting her, but she was immediately back at it. Ashlyn couldn't help but let her eyes flick to that warm, inviting pussy only a few feet away.

She tried to ignore the growing moistness between Thalia's supple thighs and the hardening nipples on the demon's sultry breasts.

"Oh my goddess, is that all you ever think about?"

Thalia gave her a mischievous smirk.

Ashlyn sighed. Okay, that was a dumb question. Of course that was all she thought about. She was a succubus.

"Hey, can you open your legs a little more," Thalia innocently requested. "So I can a better view of your adorable pussy and how wet you're getting?"

"I am not getting..."

Ashlyn stopped as she looked down and saw her pussy glistening with her juices. Shit.

"Okay, fine." She spread her legs, giving Thalia a better view. "But you have to answer my questions."

Thalia licked her lips as she gazed at Ashlyn's lovely mound.

"Anything for my favorite sexy little Half-Elf."

Ashlyn rolled her eyes. But secretly liked that Thalia thought she was so sexy.

"Why are you letting people recover from your... visits?"

"Why not?"

"That's not what succubi do."

"I'm not like most succubi."

"No kidding. You're the weirdest succubus I've ever met."

"Thank you!"

Oh boy. Ashlyn didn't know whether to be frustrated or amused by this sexy creature.

"All right, listen, you can't just go around having sex with everyone in town."

"Why not?"

"I... I don't know. You just can't!"

Ashlyn really wasn't sure why not. Having lots of super-hot sex didn't sound bad at all. And since Thalia wasn't draining their lives away like most of her kind, Ashlyn was having a harder time figuring out what to do with her.

"You just had sex before coming after me."

Ashlyn's mouth dropped.

"What?! No I... I mean... How the hell do you know that?"

"Sweetie, I'm a succubus. I can smell it on you."

She took in a big whiff.

"With some incredibly hunky local farmhand if I'm not mistaken."

Ashlyn's mouth dropped even more.

"Oh c'mon! There's no way you could know that."

"What can I say? I'm good. Wanna tell me all about it?"

"No."

"Oh c'mon, you have me tied up, so I can't touch you, which I want to do so badly. You can at least regale me with your super-slutty sexcapades."

"I was not a slut!"

"Oh you totally were. I can tell deep down you love being a submissive little slut."

"Thalia!"

"Ashlyn!"

Ashlyn folded her arms and pouted, not amused that this stupid, super-hot succubus was making fun of her.

Thalia smiled.

"Oh stop pouting, submissive sluts are my favorite people in the world. You can be submissive and still be an amazing, kick-ass demon hunter. Which you obviously are because you resisted my charms. No one has ever done that before. I'm impressed."

Ashlyn was a little surprised Thalia was admitting all that.

"Oh... well, thanks."

"Now tell me all about the super-hot sex you had with the strapping farmhand."

Ashlyn sighed. She kind of did want to tell someone about it.

"Okay, fine."

Thalia's face brightened like she was receiving the best present ever.

Ashlyn recounted how the Lavellan had burned her clothes off and she wound up naked at Corvan's farm and proceeded to have sex with him. A lot.

She noticed Thalia get wetter the more of the tale she heard. And Ashlyn realized the same thing was happening to her.

Thalia made her describe in exact detail all the different things she did and asked ridiculously personal questions.

"How big was his cock?"

"Thalia!"

"What position made you feel like the biggest whore?"

"Thalia!!"

"How much delicious farmhand cum did he shoot into that amazing, scrumptious, super-tight cunt of yours?"

"Thalia!!!"

"What? This is all important information for me to know. It helps me best know how to ravish you."

Ashlyn rolled her eyes again.

"Oh, you're going to ravish me, are you? That's going to be a little tough with you tied up."

"Not so much."

She moved her hands in front of her and displayed the untied ropes.

Ashlyn gaped at her unbound wrists. What the…?

Before she could blink, Thalia drew her into the most sensual kiss of Ashlyn's life. Putting all the other kisses Thalia had given her previously to shame.

Ashlyn lost all sense of time and space. She was consumed by Thalia's kiss and embrace. There was nothing except her.

When she regained her senses, she found herself lying on her back on an old bed in the room, her wrists tied to the bed post above her and her ankles bound with her legs spread apart.

What the hell just happened?

She saw Thalia lounging on her side, mere inches from her.

"Thalia… what… how…"

"Did you get tied up and be totally at my mercy? Oh that's easy. I used my tail to undo the rope, entranced you with my amazing succubus wiles, and then tied you up like a good little slut."

"Thalia, let me go!"

"Why would I do that when you worked so hard to make sure I would capture you like this?"

"What… what are you talking about?"

"Ashlyn, I know you left my tail unbound so I'd be able to

free myself."

"No... no I didn't."

"C'mon now. You said it yourself. You're extremely good at what you do. You wouldn't make a mistake like that. You just didn't want to admit to me that you wanted me to dominate you."

"I... I don't want..."

"So you don't want me to do this?"

Thalia slid her hand down Ashlyn's smooth stomach, across her curvy hip, and down her inner thigh.

"I... ohhh."

"Or this?"

She moved her hand over Ashlyn's left breast, squeezing her succulent nipple.

"We can't... oooo."

"How about this?"

Her hand journeyed between Ashlyn's legs and discovered her wetness.

"Uhhhhhhh!"

Thalia smiled. "I'll take that to mean you'd like me to keep going."

Ashlyn nodded despite herself, and Thalia slid into her womanhood like she owned it.

Ashlyn gasped and arched her back. Somehow Thalia immediately found all the places inside her that gave her the most intense pleasure.

She pulled against her bonds and moaned loudly.

"Oh goddess!"

Thalia climbed on top of her while plunging her fingers deeper.

"Would you like me to kiss you again?"

"Fuck yes!" Ashlyn exclaimed without even thinking about it.

Thalia brought her supple lips to Ashlyn's and found the Half-Elf extremely eager to kiss her. She let the succubus slip her long sinuous tongue into her and twist it in the most marvelous ways around her own tongue.

Ashlyn gasped into Thalia's mouth as the demon continued her expert exploration of Ashlyn's tight cavern. Thalia's fingers felt so good inside her. She was doing things to her pussy that she didn't think were possible.

Thalia's other hand moved between Ashlyn's breasts, tweaking her nipples in ways that made them ridiculously erect and feel like they were on fire.

"Ohhhhhhh!" she yelled. She knew she shouldn't be getting it on with a sneaky demon, but gods it felt so good. Her whole body felt inflamed with desire. She wanted Thalia more than anything.

Thalia had a huge smile on her face. She obviously enjoyed her work immensely, and all of Ashlyn's sexy groans were making her very happy.

She pulled away from Ashlyn's mouth, leaving her sweet saliva on Ashlyn's lips. She stared into the bound woman's emerald eyes, leaving her lips just inches away.

"I can do the most amazing things to elf ears," she cooed.

Ashlyn gazed up into the intense, violet eyes above her and knew she was going to completely give herself over to the demon, consequences be damned.

"Would you like me to show you?" Thalia purred, stroking Ashlyn's silky auburn hair.

"Yes," Ashlyn groaned as Thalia found a particular sensitive spot inside her pussy.

She felt Thalia's supple tongue find the curve of her ear and weave its way inside it. It played along all the crevices of Ashlyn's ridiculously sensitive ears, making her scream and writhe in passion.

What Thalia was doing to her ears, her tits, and her pussy was beyond anything Ashlyn had experienced.

She thrashed on the bed harder and harder, her bound limbs the only thing keeping her from flipping off it. Being tied up and ravished by Thalia was driving her crazy with desire. She never wanted Thalia to stop.

The succubus began to grind on top of her, her own passion building the more Ashlyn moaned.

"I can feel your orgasm building. Do you want to cum for me?"

"Fuck yes! I need to cum so bad!"

Just as she felt she was on the verge, Thalia turned down the intensity of what she was doing, though she still lightly manipulated all of Ashlyn's erogenous zones.

"I'll let you cum but you have to beg me for it and tell me what a good little slut you are."

Godammit. Ashlyn hated this fucking succubus. She didn't want to give in to her. But she also wanted her more than anything else in her life.

And she was so close to cumming she could barely think about anything else.

"Ohhh, fuck. Just let me cum you freaking evil, sexy demon."

"Evil? I'm so offended," Thalia said in mock indignation. "But I do like the sexy part. Just tell me what I want to hear, and I'll give you the most amazing orgasms of your entire life."

She was still exploring all of Ashlyn's sensitive body parts, keeping her on the verge of cumming without actually letting her crest the peak.

"N… no," Ashlyn whimpered, her pride fighting with her desire.

Thalia stroked her hair.

"Sweetie, I know you want to submit to me. I can sense it.

Just let yourself go. I promise I'll take care of you, and I'll cuddle with you afterward."

She kissed Ashlyn sweetly on her cute Half-Elf nose. That pretty much sealed it for Ashlyn. She had never heard of a succubus being this sweet and caring. And they definitely didn't cuddle after sex. Ashlyn really liked cuddling, though she might not admit it too often. She had a tough demon hunter persona to uphold.

Something inside her was telling her she could trust this sensual succubus. So she gave the demon what she wanted.

"Oh gods, please let me cum! I need you so bad and I'll be your fucking slut forever."

She couldn't believe she just screamed that. She felt so dirty. But also kind of good.

Thalia kissed her lovingly and squeezed her tightly.

"Yes! You really know how to make a succubus happy."

Thalia returned to her intense attack on Ashlyn's ears, tits, and pussy, this time also paying close attention to her extremely sensitive clit, squeezing and rubbing it in ways that sent Ashlyn over the edge.

She came like a volcano. Her Half-Elf juices squirting out of her and her body spasming out of control.

She let out the loudest moan of her life as her orgasms consumed her.

As she continued to shriek and squirt, she felt Thalia's tail move up her leg and thigh and find her ass. And then pierce Ashlyn's tight hole.

Holy shit! Ashlyn was completely unprepared for that. She could honestly say she never had a tail up her ass before.

But it brought her orgasms to a whole new level. She screamed in abandon, her ass muscles contracting around Thalia's sexy tail, which felt so tight inside her. While, at the same time, the demon pillaged her pussy and clit and made

Ashlyn's entire body a frenzy of orgasmic energy.

Ashlyn continued to cum. Orgasm after orgasm washed over her. Her sexy girl juices continued to flow out of her.

When she was finally done, Thalia untied her and held her tightly, as mini-orgasms made her body twitch.

She curled up against Thalia, seeking shelter in the succubus's warmth.

"That... that was incredible," Ashlyn said breathlessly.

Thalia stroked her ears and hair. "See, being with a succubus isn't so bad."

Ashlyn covered her face and groaned. "Ugh, I'm supposed to be capturing you, not letting you have your way with me."

Thalia brushed her cheek. "C'mon, isn't my way much more fun?"

The way she was embracing Ashlyn, it was hard to argue with that.

"Okay, fine, yes. But after this we need to go back to fighting each other."

"You mean after lots more amazing sex?"

"Yes."

"Okay!"

Thalia was so cheery about it, Ashlyn couldn't help but smile a little.

"You really are the weirdest succubus ever."

"Thank you!"

Ashlyn sighed. Then gazed down Thalia's amazing body. "So, um, can I..."

"Pleasure my pussy and lap up all my super-tasty succubus cum?"

"Thalia!"

"Yes you absolutely can."

Before Ashlyn could argue, Thalia had flipped her onto her knees and laid back on the bed, positioning Ashlyn so her ass was in the air and her mouth between Thalia's legs, above the most inviting lips Ashlyn had ever seen.

Ashlyn sighed again. Well, this was exactly what she was about to ask Thalia. It was uncanny the way she knew all the ultra-sexy things Ashlyn wanted to do. Must be her super-succubus powers.

She dove into Thalia's luscious lips, licking up and down her slit and playing her tongue all around it.

The succubus gyrated her hips above her and grabbed her own tits as she moaned wickedly. Ashlyn liked that she was turning such a sexual creature on so much.

She got her second taste of Thalia's succulent juices and they tasted even more delicious than the first time.

"Mmm, you taste so good."

Thalia grabbed Ashlyn's hair with one hand and thrust her face farther into her moistening pussy.

"Oh yes! Lap it all up you sexy Half-Elf slut."

Ashlyn didn't know how Thalia was making her enjoy being called a slut so much, but she renewed her exploration of Thalia's tight pleasure hole with even more vigor.

Thalia's pussy seemed to squeeze and caress her tongue as she entered her. Holy shit. Ashlyn had been inside plenty of lovely girls' folds but none of them had a pussy like Thalia's.

Her tongue seemed made to be inside the succubus and she couldn't help but want to explore every inch of the ridiculously tight cavern.

Thalia's juices seeped into her mouth, which made her want to fuck the demon even harder.

Thalia writhed on top of her.

"Oh Ashlyn! Your tongue belongs inside me. Fuck me you little whore and make me unload all my demon cum into your needy mouth."

By the gods, could Thalia be any more dirty or make

Ashlyn feel like a bigger slut? And, dammit, why did Ashlyn like it so much?

She reached underneath Thalia and grabbed her ass. Oh goddess. She had never touched a more perfect specimen of flesh.

Thalia turned on her side, giving Ashlyn better access to her phenomenal posterior. Ashlyn kneaded her fingers into the supple purple skin and didn't want to let go. As she did, Thalia wrapped her legs around Ashlyn's head and tugged her hair again, making sure she got as deep as possible inside her pussy. With Thalia's thighs holding her in place, Ashlyn had no choice but to pleasure the succubus until she decided she had cum enough into her mouth. Ashlyn was more than happy to oblige and absorbed herself in Thalia's delicious pussy, which seemed to be massaging her tongue and inviting her to search out every crevice of it.

"Fuck yes!" Thalia moaned. "Stroke the base of my tail. It's super-sensitive."

The tail was thickest near Thalia's ass. Definitely wider than a cock. Ashlyn wrapped both hands around it and stroked it gently.

"Oo yeah, just like that sweetie. But you can go harder."

Ashlyn complied, jerking Thalia off harder as she continued to tongue fuck her.

She must have been doing a good job, as she could feel Thalia's tail whip around, reacting to the pleasure her body was receiving.

Thalia rotated them back to their original position, with her on her back and Ashlyn on her knees with her lovely ass in the air. Thalia lifted her legs to give Ashlyn easy access to her tail, which Ashlyn continue to stroke hard. But kept one hand on Ashlyn's hair, making sure the Half-Elf's lips never left her delectable mound.

The tail played along Ashlyn's ass and then spanked her. Her moan was muffled because she was buried deep within Thalia's luscious folds.

Thalia spanked her again. Harder. Fuck. Getting her ass slapped by a sexy succubus tail was turning Ashlyn on more than she expected.

After several more delicious spankings, she felt the end of Thalia's tail brush across her pussy lips and then enter her.

She gasped into Thalia's mound. The new sensation of having a tail inside her pussy was amazing. It wormed around inside her, flicking at the parts of her that made her squirm in ecstasy.

And it was so long it easily filled her all the way to her cervix.

"Ohhhh Thalia!"

Thalia pushed Ashlyn's mouth back onto her pussy. She obviously really wanted Ashlyn to make her cum. It was only fair after the million orgasms she had given Ashlyn.

Ashlyn licked Thalia's clit, which was larger and more pronounced than a normal woman's. She had plenty to suck on and play with and she worked it hard, loving the sultry sounds coming out of the succubus.

Thalia alternated using her tail to fuck Ashlyn's tight pussy and even tighter ass. The succubus had amazing command of her tail, using it to perfection to make Ashlyn utter the sluttiest moans.

Ashlyn and Thalia's screams created a sultry symphony of ecstasy and they both came at the same time. Thalia's sweet cum flowed into Ashlyn's mouth and she happily lapped it up. She couldn't believe it tasted so good. No wonder everyone wanted to have sex with succubi.

At the same time, Ashlyn's own nectar was spurting out of her all over Thalia's tail, which was plunging Ashlyn's depths for all they were worth.

After lots of screaming and moaning, Ashlyn collapsed on top of Thalia, both their chests heaving.

Thalia brought her tail up to her mouth and sucked Ashlyn's juices off it, purring in delight. Apparently, she enjoyed the taste of Ashlyn just as much as Ashlyn loved Thalia's sweetness.

She then wiped the tail across Ashlyn's cheek, smearing it and Ashlyn's lips with her own cum. Ashlyn was going to object but as this point, why not go all the way. She sucked her own cum off Thalia's tail, creating a sweet and salty mixture with Thalia's nectar that was already on her tongue.

Thalia smiled at her.

"How does it feel to be a naughty slut?"

Ashlyn made a face at her.

"I hate you."

"What? You think I'm the most desirable creature in the world and you want to cuddle with me until morning?"

Great. How did she get the succubus with a wacky sense of humor?

She sighed. "Okay, fine. Let's cuddle."

Thalia turned Ashlyn on her side and wrapped her up from behind, her arms, legs, and tail enveloping her in a way that made Ashlyn feel like she didn't want to be anywhere else.

She sighed again, but this time with complete contentment.

She felt Thalia nuzzle into her neck and warm breath brush against her skin. It felt really nice.

Shit. She really hoped she wasn't falling for this succubus.

She drifted off to sleep as Thalia gently caressed her.

CHAPTER THREE

Ashlyn stirred from her very restful sleep, feeling the most perfectly warm and curvy body against her.

Her eyes fluttered open and she saw Thalia's body draped over her, the succubus staring at her.

"Good morning!" the demon said cheerfully.

Ashlyn got lost in her eyes. "Hi... were you watching me sleep?"

"Yes. You're adorable when you're not yelling at me or threatening to vanquish me to the underworld."

Ashlyn wrinkled her cute Half-Elf nose, which Thalia promptly kissed.

"I did not threaten to vanquish you to the underworld."

"Well sure not after we had the most amazing sex in the five lands."

Ashlyn blushed. It actually might qualify for that.

Thalia was softly caressing Ashlyn's body as they talked, making Ashlyn very relaxed.

"I can't believe we did that."

Thalia gave Ashlyn one of her trademark mischievous grins.

"I can!"

Ashlyn gave her a pretend dirty look. Then realized

something.

"Hey. You didn't try to drain my sexual energy last night."

"Yup."

"Why not?"

"Why do you think?"

"I don't know. You confuse the hell out of me."

Thalia continued to trace sexy patterns along Ashlyn's skin until her fingers reached Ashlyn's soft lips.

"Maybe I really like you."

She kissed Ashlyn intimately.

Ashlyn was even more confused. She had never heard of a succubus having romantic feelings for someone. It was all about sex with them. Did Thalia want a relationship with her? Shit this was one weird succubus. But one Ashlyn couldn't help but admit she was liking more and more the longer they spent together.

Before she could examine her feelings further, she realized something else. She was tied to the bed again. What the hell? She had no idea how she was just realizing this now. Dammit, she must have been so focused on Thalia she wasn't thinking of anything else. This succubus was really doing a number on her.

"Um, how did I get tied up?"

"Oh, I did it when I woke up and you were still sleeping. I'm really good at stealthy bondage."

"Okay. Why am I tied up?"

"So you can't chase after me."

"What?!"

Thalia tousled Ashlyn's soft hair.

"In case your demon hunter nobleness gets the better of you, I want to make sure I have plenty of time to escape."

"What about all that stuff about really liking me?"

She kissed Ashlyn on the cheek.

"I do really like you sweetie. But I'm still a succubus and I need to be mischievous. And leaving you tied up naked while I skedaddle brings me all kinds of pleasure."

"Well it doesn't bring me pleasure you nutcase. Let me go!"

"Oh c'mon, think about how much fun it will be to hunt me down again and how much better it will make the sex."

"Thalia, you are not leaving me like this!"

Thalia gave her a warm kiss on the lips, squeezed her tits, then climbed off her.

"Thalia!" She struggled against her bonds.

The succubus lifted her tail and swayed her hips, giving Ashlyn a phenomenal view of her jiggling ass and making her wet.

Ashlyn pulled even harder against the ropes, but she couldn't get free.

"Thalia I will kick your ass so hard if you don't untie me right now!"

The demon blew her a kiss.

"See you soon my sexy demon hunter."

And with that she disappeared out the window.

"Thalia!!"

She thrashed around some more and then finally realized she was just tiring herself out.

Stupid, mischievous, pain in the ass, ultra sexy succubus. Who left her wet and wanting to be fucked. Ugh, how did she get herself into these messes?

Better yet, how was she going to get out of it? She slowed her breathing, trying to focus and work more deliberately at her bonds. She felt a little bit of play in the ropes. She could get out of them, but it was going to take a while.

It didn't help that she kept thinking about how hot it was that she was tied up, completely naked and helpless. And how much she would love Thalia to come back and ravish her. But after that she would totally kick her ass.

*****

After an hour of working at the ropes, she heard a noise from the floor below. Shit. Someone was in the house. And if it wasn't Thalia, this was going to be super-embarrassing.

She went faster, trying to will her bonds to release her. She was almost free when the door to the room crashed open.

And Corvan rushed in.

Ashlyn was equal parts surprised, excited, and relieved to see him.

But then she was more parts super-embarrassed as she saw the look on his face at seeing her naked and bound.

"Oh my…"

He rushed over to her.

"Are you okay? Did someone hurt you? If they did, I'll…"

She smiled. He was so sweet.

"I'm totally fine. Except my pride."

He looked relieved.

"So what…"

"Please don't ask."

"Ashlyn, you're naked and tied to a bed and your…"

His gaze traveled down her body to between her legs.

She glanced down. Shit. She was still fucking wet.

"Okay fine, I was chasing that succubus you told me about and I thought I had her but she was super-weird and sexy and she tied me up and made me be all submissive to her and say ridiculously slutty things and I came a lot. And then she left me like this."

She took a huge breath after her non-stop confession was over. She was afraid to look at Corvan.

She finally peeked at him and saw he was sitting there

dumbfounded.

"Um, could you say something?"

"Wow."

"Say something else!"

"What am I supposed to say?"

"I don't know! Yell at me for being seduced by that stupid succubus. For letting her tie me up like her sex toy."

"Well, you do look incredibly sexy like that."

"Corvan!"

He massaged her thigh gently.

"Ashlyn, I'm not going to yell at you. I didn't expect you to never sleep with anyone else. I wasn't even sure when I would see you again. I mean I am kind of jealous you had such amazing sex with her, but that doesn't change the way I feel about you."

"How... how do you feel about me?"

He leaned down and gave her one of the most loving, passionate kisses of her life.

"Does that answer your question?"

"Uh huh."

She smiled up at him.

"I'm so glad you're here. But how did you find me?"

"Oh, yeah it was very strange. There was a note on our door saying you were in trouble and where you were. So I rushed over as fast as I could."

Ashlyn kissed him again.

"My hero."

As he blushed, Ashlyn realized Thalia must have told Corvan where to find her. So that sneaky succubus wasn't quite as bad as Ashlyn thought. But she was still going to get it when Ashlyn tracked her down.

Corvan reached for the rope around her nearest wrist. Ashlyn bit her lip, feeling very naughty.

"Wait."

"What's wrong?"

"Before you untie me, do you maybe want to…"

She raised her eyebrow at him.

"I… didn't realize you were so kinky."

"Me either. So can you please fuck me now?"

"Yes ma'am."

He removed his clothes and lowered his dark, muscular body on top of her. She felt his impressive cock immediately get rock hard against her. It had only been a day, but she couldn't wait for it to be inside her again.

His lips found hers and they kissed tenderly as he caressed her breasts and made her nipples get very erect.

"Oh Corvan I need you inside me. I'm completely at your mercy."

Okay, so she was really getting into this submissive stuff. And she could see Corvan was getting very turned on by her dirty talk.

She felt his huge shaft enter her wetness.

"Ohhhh!" she gasped as her taut arms and legs pulled against her bindings.

It slid into her perfectly and filled her completely.

"Uhh, your pussy is amazing."

"Please fuck me and make me cum!"

He thrust in and out of her and swirled his tongue around her ears in the way she loved. Even though they had just met yesterday, they had made love so many times, they knew each others' bodies very intimately.

Ashlyn moved her hips in rhythm to Corvan's throbbing cock, which was making her pussy so freaking wet.

"Oh gods, fuck me harder!"

He increased his pace. His powerful groans mixing with her sultry moans. He felt so good piercing her folds, touching every part of her insides. Setting off tiny fires within her.

His strong hands did wonders to her tits and his tongue switched between kissing her waiting lips and licking her sensitive ears.

"Oh goddess, Corvan make me your elven slut!"

That got him to really plow into her. Making her utter non-stop moans, whimpers, and screams.

She pulled hard against her bonds as her body writhed under him and as he clasped her tightly.

Her shrieks intensified until she let loose the loudest one yet as her orgasm overwhelmed her.

"Ohhhhhhahhhhhhh!"

As she was cumming, she felt Corvan's body and cock tighten up and then he unloaded his sweet seed into her. She squealed louder as she felt it fill her tight pussy.

Their sexy sounds reverberated off the walls until he collapsed on top of her, both of them panting and his cock still inside her.

"Wow," he breathed into her neck.

"Uh huh," she managed to get out.

She peered over his shoulder.

"What are you looking for?"

"Oh, nothing. I was half expecting your Mom to walk in on us like she did all those other times."

He propped himself up and smiled at her.

"Well she usually does that while we're in the middle of it, not after we're done."

She smiled back.

"That's true."

"Oh that reminds me."

He scooted off the bed and rummaged through his pack, coming back to the bed with a wrapped box.

"My Mom sent a present for you."

Ashlyn loved Rima so much. And she had just met her yesterday.

"That's really sweet."

She looked up at her bonds.

"Can you untie me?"

Corvan looked like he was thinking it over.

"Well..."

"Corvannnn."

He grinned and undid her wrist and ankle bonds. He helped her rub them and get the blood flowing.

She tore open the box like she used to do when getting presents during the Blossom Festival.

Her eyes went wide and she turned very red when she saw they were a pair of extremely skimpy lavender panties.

"Oh..."

She peeked at Corvan and he was even redder.

"I... I swear I didn't know what was in there."

She could see how embarrassed he was. She stroked his arm.

"Oh c'mon. She just wants us to be together. It's kind of romantic."

"It's kind of mortifying."

"So you're saying you don't want me to try these on?"

She ran her fingers through the soft fabric and licked her lips.

"Um, no, I'm definitely not saying that."

"Okay, turn around."

"Why? You're already naked."

She whacked him on the shoulder.

"Because it will ruin the allure you nitwit."

He gave her a look like he didn't understand women but turned around.

She slipped the panties up her smooth legs slowly, enjoying

the feel of the fabric against her tanned skin. When she got them all the way up, they just barely covered her pussy and the thinnest piece of material fit tightly between her ass cheeks, leaving virtually nothing to the imagination.

She blushed at thinking of Rima picking these out for her. She was a unique mom that was for sure.

She tried out a couple of sexy poses, decided most of them were more awkward than sexy, and finally settled on one with her hip stuck out and her hands above and behind her head.

"O... okay, you can turn around."

She wasn't used to wearing sexy stuff or posing provocatively, so she hoped she was doing it right.

Corvan faced her and his mouth dropped. He just stood there, staring at her.

Ashlyn blushed furiously. Apparently she was doing it right.

"Will you say something?"

"Wow."

"Say something else!"

"You're the sexiest, most beautiful creature I've ever seen in my life."

Ashlyn blushed even more furiously.

"Oh, um, thanks."

"Could you..."

He made a motion for her to spin around.

She rolled her eyes but secretly wanted to show off her hot ass in the skimpy garment.

She turned and stuck her perky ass out, shaking it for him.

"Oh gods! Ashlyn you're making me want to take you again right now."

She looked slyly over her shoulder.

"Well, what are you waiting for?"

He took her in his arms and was kissing her neck, shoulder,

and lips as his hands traveled down and found her ass that was so prominently on display.

She gasped into his mouth as he squeezed. Rima's present was definitely having the desired effect.

His hands moved up her body, across her luscious tits, and then down to her panties.

He slowly slid them off her wettening mound and down her toned legs.

She stepped out of them, but before he could toss them aside, she got another super-naughty idea.

She put her hand on his and the panties.

"Wait, I think there's another use for these."

She thrust her wrists out together in front of her.

It took him a minute but then it dawned on him. His eyes lit up.

He wrapped the skimpy underwear around her wrists and used them to bind her hands together.

Fuck. She got wet as soon as he did. Being tied up with her own slutty panties was turning her on like crazy.

There was a chandelier hanging from the low ceiling and Corvan attached the panties to it, so her hands were stuck above her head.

She got even wetter.

"Um, you're getting pretty good at this," she told him.

"Well, it helps when you have a super-sexy Half-Elf ass to fuck."

"Corvan!"

He rubbed his head sheepishly.

"Oh sorry. I was trying to talk dirty. I thought you liked that."

"No, I... I do. You're just... so sweet I wasn't expecting it."

"I wasn't expecting you to want me to tie you up with your underwear."

Okay, good point.

"Okay fine, fuck me like a dirty little slut."

He spanked her, eliciting a yelp. He slapped her ass again, harder. She was powerless to stop him, but he knew she loved it when he played with her ass.

After making her hot from being spanked, he clasped her hips and ran his huge shaft up and down between her cheeks.

She wiggled her butt, wanting him to stop teasing her and give her the fucking she deserved.

He finally did, inserting his head between her soft lips and sliding it all the way into her up to its hilt.

She gasped in pleasure. She absolutely loved it when he fucked her from behind. He was able to get so deep inside her.

He rammed her good. Sending shockwaves of bliss through her core every time he speared her.

He reached around and grasped her tits as he fucked her, rubbing her nipples in ways that sent tingles through her breasts and down her stomach to the even larger sensations happening between her legs.

She felt the texture of her panties rub against her wrists as they kept her from moving and left her in the sexy position with her back arched, her ass stuck out, and her tits thrust forward. While Corvan continued to thread her tight, sensitive folds.

He lowered one of his hands to her clit and squeezed it just the right amount for maximum pleasure while he plunged all the way into her from behind.

She came hard. Splattering her thighs and legs with her cum and coating Corvan's massive cock.

Her pussy tightened around him and made him explode inside her, a huge amount of his sexy man juice squirting into her.

He shot his seed into her a bunch more times as she

squirted out more of her sweet juices.

When they were both finally spent, he unhooked her from the chandelier and they collapsed onto the floor in a heap. He wrapped his arms around her from behind and held her against him. Her wrists were still bound by her panties, but she kind of liked that.

She sighed as he peppered the back of her neck with sweet kisses.

"So we should tell your mom we put her gift to good use," she teased.

"We are definitely not telling her that."

"It would make her really happy."

"Ashlyn!"

"Okay, fine. But you have to thank her for me. It was really sweet of her."

"I'll do that. Without any of the explicit details."

"Okay." She nuzzled against him closer. Suddenly, she wasn't mad at all that Thalia had left her tied up. She actually did her a favor, letting her have more time with Corvan. Not that she was going to admit that to the conniving succubus.

They lay there for a while, content to just be in each others' arms.

When they finally got up, Ashlyn reluctantly relented and told Corvan more about her adventures with Thalia.

"She stuck her tail where?"

"Corvan! It's embarrassing enough without having to repeat it."

"But I think getting the details of this part are really important."

She punched him in the arm as he smirked at her.

"I'm telling your mom you're making fun of me."

"Well, I'm telling her you had sex with a succubus."

"Don't you dare!"

She leapt onto him and wrestled him to the ground, twisting his arm behind his back.

"Ah! Ashlyn!"

"Swear you won't tell her."

"I swear! I swear!"

She let him go. He rubbed his arm.

"I was just kidding."

She looked at him contritely.

"Sorry. It's just… it's important what your mom thinks of me. I don't… want her to think…"

"That you love banging demons?"

She was about to punch him again when he held up his hands in surrender.

"I'm joking."

He moved closer and clasped her arms.

"Ashlyn, my mom adores you. She hasn't stopped talking about you since you left. She would probably adopt you if she could."

"Re… really?"

"Really. And she's not the only one who adores you."

He gave her that smile she loved so much. She smiled back and hugged him tightly.

"You're a good man Corvan."

She pulled back a little so she could look at him.

"But you cannot tell anyone I slept with a succubus."

He took her hands. "You have my word."

She kissed him.

"But can I tell them how much you love being tied up and treated like a slut?"

"Okay that's it!"

She tackled him and they wrestled playfully on the floor until he was inside her again, warming her with his wonderful manhood.

*****

When they were finally done with all the sex, she let him dress her. He helped her into her new, skimpy panties, then pulled her leggings up over her hips and her tunic over her head.

She touched him fondly as he did, liking that he was so gentle in how he dressed her.

He pulled her into him, her arms pressed against his well-defined chest. He squeezed her ass affectionately as they kissed lovingly.

"So you know that thing she did with her tail…"

"Oh goddess, you want to fuck me up my ass too?"

He looked chagrined. "Only if you're okay with it. I don't want to… You know what, forget it, I shouldn't have…"

"Oh stop, it's fine. I was thinking about it too. Okay, yes, you can fuck me up my tight Half-Elf ass. But you'll have to wait until next time I see you. I have to find Thalia before she gets too much of a head start."

"You have yourself a date."

She smiled. "Well, you better romance me first before you plunder my ass."

"I already have something in mind," he replied with a twinkle in his eye.

She kissed him sweetly.

"I can't wait."

CHAPTER FOUR

Ashlyn tracked Thalia down in Spring Meadow, the next town over. It wasn't hard to find her. She just had to look for the angry mob who looked like they wanted to burn her at the stake.

She was cornered in an alley. The townsfolk yelling curses at her and blaming her for ruining their marriages.

Ashlyn peered down at her from the rooftop above. Oh Thalia. The troublesome succubus had really gotten herself into it this time.

Thalia was backing away from the advancing mob, running out of room really quickly. She was trying to look confident, but Ashlyn could tell she was scared.

Succubi were good at using their charms on one or two people. Maybe even a few. But not over a dozen. And not when they were carrying weapons and threatening to use them.

Ashlyn sighed. Obviously she had to save the big dummy. Stupid succubus.

One irate man hurled a dagger at Thalia. Ashlyn swooped down, caught the dagger in mid-air, and landed in a graceful crouch.

She hurled the dagger back at the man, knocking off his

pretentious hat, the dagger fastening it to the wall of the house.

The mob stopped as Ashlyn gave them her classic demon hunter glare. She then spun behind Thalia and tied her hands behind her back.

Thalia gazed into her eyes, relieved and grateful.

"I am so happy to see you."

"You owe me big time for this," Ashlyn whispered in her ear. "Now just play along."

She moved to the side of Thalia.

"Good townspeople. I am Demon Hunter Ashlyn. I've been pursuing this succubus across many towns. Thank you for your help in apprehending her."

"Kill her!" someone from the crowd yelled.

"Burn her!" another pacifist screamed.

Ashlyn held up her hands, trying to quiet them.

"I have bound her with the Rope of... Chastity. She is powerless against it and will no longer be able to have sex."

She nudged Thalia. The sexy demon fell to her knees, yelling in mock pain.

"Argghh! No!! Not the Rope of Chastity. Anything but that! I can't survive without copious amounts of lurid, sinful sex!"

Ashlyn tried to keep a straight face. This idiot was really playing it up.

Thalia thrashed on the ground.

"Ohhhh, please sexy demon hunter, unbind me so I can fuck every single person in this town a million times."

Ashlyn kicked her. Not too hard but enough to tell her to knock off the overly dramatic theatrics.

She turned to the crowd.

"As you can see folks, the succubus has been rendered harmless and-"

"Get her while she's helpless!" they yelled.

"What?!" Thalia sat up like a shot, her terrible pain suddenly gone.

Well, so much for Ashlyn's great plan. She scanned the alley as the mob rushed them. Thalia leapt up and hid behind Ashlyn.

She saw a window cart halfway up the house. It was used to lift heavy objects or goods up to higher floors via windows instead of carrying them up flights of stairs.

Ashlyn hurled her dagger at one of the ropes attached to the cart. It cut cleanly through it and the cart lurched to a skewed angle, spilling the large bags of flour on it.

The white powder dumped all over the townsfolk, creating a summer winter wonderland. They sputtered and coughed as the flour got in their noses and mouths.

"C'mon!" Ashlyn yelled.

She snatched Thalia's arm, still tied behind her, and pulled her through the crowd.

They got covered in the powder as they barged their way through, kicking and elbowing irate flour-clad people out of the way.

"Really great plan Ashlyn," Thalia complained.

"It would have been great except for someone's idiotic dramatics."

"Hey! I think I should get an acting award for that."

"Oh shut up and let me save your super-sexy ass."

Thalia shut up, apparently appeased that Ashlyn thought her ass was so alluring.

They forced their way through the rest of the mob and rushed out of the alley. Ashlyn led Thalia down a maze of different streets, finally losing their pursuers.

As they hid behind a horse barn, they gazed at each other. They laughed, realizing how ridiculous they both looked coated in flour.

Ashlyn found some buckets of water and dumped one of them over Thalia.

"Ahh! Ashlyn that's freezing!"

Ashlyn dumped another one on her.

"Ahhh! Would you stop?"

Ashlyn stepped back, gazing at the water running down Thalia's ultra-sensual body, over her erect nipples, down her taut stomach, and across her curvy hips and thighs. It was even more alluring with Thalia's hands bound behind her back.

Ashlyn immediately dumped a cold bucket of water over her own head. Both to clean herself off and to dampen the burning desire growing between her legs.

She flung her wet hair back and saw Thalia staring at the way her soaked clothes clung to her now partially visible tits and shapely legs.

She brushed the wet hair out of Thalia's face and kissed her.

"I like you all wet."

"I need to rip all your clothes off right now and fuck you," Thalia informed her.

Ashlyn smirked at her. "Okay, let's get a room."

*****

Ashlyn snuck them into an empty room in an inn on the other side of town. She flung Thalia onto the comfy bed and tied her hands and legs to the bedpost, this time making sure to bind her tail too.

Even though she was bound, Thalia still managed to position herself in the sexiest way possible.

"Oh no! You've tied me up with the Rope of Chastity. Whatever will I do?"

Ashlyn stuck her tongue out at the annoying demon.

"Hey, it's the first thing I thought of all right. And I was trying to save your stupid, sexy butt. I should have let them burn you at the stake."

"Oh c'mon, then how would we have super-naughty sex all day and night?"

Ashlyn wrung her tunic out, pretending to ignore her.

Thalia was silent for a while, then finally sighed.

"Ashlyn..." she began hesitantly.

Ashlyn turned, seeing a genuineness on Thalia's face she hadn't seen before.

"Thank you for saving me. It... it was really nice of you. I... I was actually really scared, and I don't know what I would have done if you hadn't shown up. So, um, yeah thanks."

Ashlyn looked at Thalia like she was seeing her for the first time. The succubus was being... sweet. There was more to her than Ashlyn thought. Thalia really just needed a friend.

She silently walked over and sat on the bed. Leaned over and kissed Thalia sweetly.

"You're welcome. I suppose you're not so bad. For a succubus."

"Yes! I knew you loved me."

Ashlyn rolled her eyes but also smiled.

"Um, so can you untie me now?"

"Nope."

"Why not?"

"Because you left me tied up in a decrepit house totally naked, that's why you idiot! So now I'm returning the favor."

She smirked at the bound succubus.

"Oh c'mon, you love being tied up. It lets you act out all your dirty, slutty fantasies."

Ashlyn tried not to blush. It was so annoying that Thalia knew her kinky fetishes so well.

"And anyway," the succubus continued. "I made sure you got to have super-amazing submissive sex with your hunky farmhand. And I waited outside until he got there to make sure you were okay."

"You… you did?"

"Well, yeah. I like you."

Ashlyn softened. Dammit, how was she supposed to stay mad at this sneaky demon when she was being so nice?

"So obviously you should be thanking me for giving you and your farmboy lover an amazing fuck fest. Don't tell me it wasn't amazing."

Ashlyn smiled, remembering everything she did with Corvan.

"Okay yes, it was fucking awesome. I was really happy to see him. So, um, thank you."

"You're welcome! Making sure super-sexy people fuck their brains out is part of the job."

She beamed, very proud of herself.

"Okay, now will you untie me."

"Nope."

"Ashlyn!"

"I'm going to tease you for once."

She kissed Thalia on the nose. Then stood up and took a few steps away and ran her hands over her drenched clothes.

"Oh, I'm so wet. I should probably take all these soaked clothes off."

Thalia raised her head to make sure she could fully see Ashlyn.

"Oo, you should totally do that."

Ashlyn whipped her wet reddish-brown hair behind her. She was beginning to pick up some sultry moves from Thalia. Maybe the succubus wasn't such a bad influence after all.

She pulled her tunic down off her shoulders, revealing all

of her tits except her nipples.

Her top clung to her breasts, which looked even sexier than normal with the water glistening off them.

"By Shadses, please show me your wet, succulent tits!" Thalia proclaimed.

Ashlyn grinned, glad that she was turning Thalia on and making her beg to see more of her sexy Half-Elf skin.

She pulled her tunic down more, making sure her tits jiggled provocatively as her hard nipples were revealed.

Thalia moaned and pulled against her bonds.

"Oh c'mon, I need to touch you so bad."

"No touching," Ashlyn admonished her. "Just looking."

Thalia groaned. "Ugh, that's no fair."

Ashlyn continued her wet striptease. She turned around and slowly worked her drenched leggings down over her hips. She could feel the droplets run down her ridiculously sexy ass.

"Oh hells, where did you get that thong?"

Ashlyn blushed. She had forgotten she was wearing Rima's scandalous gift. The saturated fabric was stuck firmly between her two luscious cheeks.

"Oh, um, Corvan's mom gave it to me as a present."

"Best mom ever! You need to wear that all the time when you're around me. Except for when you're naked, which you need to get right now please."

Ashlyn shook her head at the horny demon but was very ready to comply with her request.

She finished removing her leggings, then played with her thong, moving it up and down, revealing parts of but not her entire ass.

She peeked over her shoulder and saw Thalia writhe against her bonds, wanting desperately to be free and take Ashlyn. She also noticed the growing wetness between the succubus's legs. And it wasn't just from the water Ashlyn had dumped on her.

She finally put the sultry demon out of her misery and pulled her thong all the way off, spanking herself a couple of times and sending rivulets of water running down her firm cheeks.

"Ohhh Ashlyn, you are so fucking hot! C'mon c'mon c'mon, let me ravish your amazing Half-Elf body."

Ashlyn climbed onto the foot of the bed and crawled up Thalia's body, almost touching it but not quite.

She got up to Thalia's face and let her tits fall just out of reach of the succubus's eager mouth.

"Uhhh, stop teasing me and let me lick your tits!"

Ashlyn kissed her on the cheek.

"Maybe later."

She hopped off the bed and scooted to the door.

"Wait? Where are you going?"

"Oh I'm famished. I'm going to get some food. Don't worry I'll be back in an hour or two."

"An hour or two?! Okay this is totally not fair. When I left you tied up, you got to have amazing sex at the end of it."

"Well maybe you will too if you're a good little demon."

She had grabbed some clothes off a clothesline on their way to the inn and now yanked them on. Then slipped out the door.

"Ashlyn!" she heard Thalia yell behind her as she snuck away, smiling.

*****

Ashlyn actually returned less than thirty minutes later, holding a yummy frozen desert in a wooden bowl.

She took off her borrowed clothes and sat next to Thalia on the bed, eating the creamy deliciousness.

Thalia pouted, still tied up.

"You know I'm supposed to be the one doing all the sexual teasing and torturing."

Ashlyn kept eating. "Uh huh."

"Succubi are not supposed to be tied up. We're supposed to do the tying."

"I think you look super-sexy this way."

"I... wait, really?"

Ashlyn whispered seductively in Thalia's ear.

"So sexy."

Thalia shivered as a pleasurable tingle ran through her.

"Hey, stop trying to distract me with my own games."

"Oh relax, you sexy little succubus. I'll let you go in a minute. Then you can tie me up and ravish me to your mischievous heart's content."

Thalia perked up. "Really?"

"Yup."

"Oh thank the gods! I mean the demons."

Ashlyn grinned at her. "You're nowhere near as evil as you want people to think."

"Shhh, don't spread that around. I have a reputation to uphold you know."

"Uh huh."

Knowing that she was going to get to slut Ashlyn up seemed to pacify Thalia. Though she still looked longingly at Ashlyn's bowl.

"Can I have some of your dessert?"

"I thought you didn't need to eat."

"I don't need to. But it doesn't mean I don't enjoy it. C'mon, please."

"Okay, open up."

Ashlyn stuck a spoonful of the sugary, creamy goodness in Thalia's mouth. She moaned in delight as it hit her tongue.

Ashlyn scooped out a bigger chunk and just happened to drop it on Thalia's boob.

"Oops."

"Hey, you did that on purpose."

"Guess I should clean that off."

She licked Thalia's breast and nipple, wiping off some of the ice cream and making Thalia shudder.

"Ohh, what... happened to letting me ravish you?"

"Oh that's totally happening. But you don't mind if I do a little research first, do you? As part of my job, I need to explore every aspect of a demon's anatomy."

"I've been such a bad influence on you."

In reply, Ashlyn plopped another blob of the frozen cream directly on Thalia's gorgeous pussy and immediately licked along her slit.

Thalia shook all over and moaned loudly.

"So that was a yes to fucking your hot demon body?"

"Yes! Fuck yes! Do whatever you want to me."

Ashlyn knew it was almost unheard of for a succubus to admit that. They were the ones making their victims scream things and beg them to drain all their sexual energy. So for all Thalia's bravado and teasing, she must feel a real connection to Ashlyn and trust her.

Ashlyn never expected to be so eager to have sex with a demon. There was part of her that was still trying to convince herself it was wrong. But that part was getting fainter and fainter. She really liked being around Thalia. The succubus was fun, and they were kind of becoming friends. And she certainly knew how to send Ashlyn to more extreme places of sexual rapture than she thought possible. Which hopefully would happen soon. But first, she needed to get down to pleasuring the amazing, sensual body underneath her.

She slid two of her fingers into Thalia's welcoming

demonhood and used her other hand to rub up and down her lovely tail.

"Ohhhhh," Thalia cried as her demon pussy clenched around Ashlyn's fingers and her tail throbbed in delight.

Thalia's perfect purple body rode Ashlyn's fingers, moving in harmony with them. Ashlyn watched her new demon friend's body undulate like sensual waves on a sea.

Both her hands were being coated in the succubus's sultry sauce, which was coming out in rhythmic timing with Thalia's moans.

"Oh hells, I've never submitted like this before."

"Wait, really?"

Ashlyn continued her pleasure-providing, and Thalia uttered sensual sounds as they talked.

"Uh huh," Thalia moaned.

"So I'm the first one you've let treat you like a demon slut?"

"Uhhhh, yes!"

Huh. Guess the not-so-evil demon really did like her.

Thalia thrashed on the bed, at the height of pleasure. Ashlyn felt her perfect pussy clench even tighter around her fingers and knew she was about to blow.

"Ohh... ohhhh... ohhhhhh... ohhhhhhhhhhh!

She came spectacularly and squirted her juices everywhere.

Ashlyn buried her face in Thalia's violet mound and sucked her clit, making her squirt even harder and drinking as much sweet succubus cum as she could.

She crawled up Thalia's body and lay on top of her, kissing her tenderly.

"So can I tell everyone you like being a demon slut?"

"Absolutely not! I'll be kicked out of the Sultry Succubus Club."

"Yeah right. Wait, do you guys really have a club?"

"Yup. We meet every week and share what devious and depraved ways we made people horny whores."

Ashlyn studied Thalia's pretty face.

"I have no idea if you're being serious."

"Yup I'm a mystery. But a really fun one to try to unravel."

Thalia kissed her nose. She had taken to doing that a lot, and Ashlyn thought it was quite sweet.

She ruffled Thalia's thick, dark hair and then ran her fingers through it, coming close to her unique features.

"Can I touch your horns?"

"Sure. They're really sensitive."

Ashlyn ran her cum-soaked fingers along the smooth curves of Thalia's horns.

"Mmm," Thalia moaned contentedly.

Ashlyn brought her lips to Thalia's as she gently stroked her horns. They kissed tenderly, Thalia making soft noises into Ashlyn's mouth as her ridges were massaged.

They did that for quite a while, getting lost in each others' mouths.

When they finally came up for air and Ashlyn had explored every curve and divot of Thalia's sexy horns, Thalia stared up at her with her bright amethyst eyes.

"I've never kissed someone that long before."

Ashlyn was flattered. As a succubus, Thalia probably normally cut right to the intense, orgasmic sex-draining activities rather than sweet smooching.

She continued to move her thumbs over Thalia's horns.

"It was nice, right?"

"Oh I suppose. You know what's also nice?"

Ashlyn sighed. "Tying me up, ravishing me, and making me the biggest slut in the five lands?"

"Yes!" Thalia exclaimed with the hugest smile Ashlyn had ever seen on her face. "You know me so well!"

Ashlyn couldn't resist that grin.

She untied Thalia and knelt in front of her.

"Okay, since I promised, go ahead and tie me up however you want and do whatever naughty demon thing you want to me."

Thalia looked like Ashlyn just told her they were going to have the most epic orgy in the history of the world.

"Are you freakin' serious?"

"Yes."

Thalia hugged her so tightly Ashlyn almost couldn't breathe.

"Oh thank you, thank you, thank you!"

Before she knew it, Ashlyn was propped up on a couple of pillows, her face down on the bed, her ass sticking up in the air, her arms bound behind her back.

Damn, Thalia didn't waste any time.

"All comfy my favorite Half-Elf slut?"

Ashlyn was actually pretty comfortable. Thalia had her arms firmly bound but not too tightly that it hurt.

"Just peachy."

"Oh good! Because I have a big surprise for you."

"You do?"

"Yup, now close your eyes."

"Thalia…"

Whap! Thalia spanked her hot ass.

"Ow!"

"Oh stop, you love it."

She gave her another good whack. Okay, so Ashlyn did love it.

After a half-dozen more spankings, Ashlyn gave in.

"Okay, okay, I'm closing my eyes."

Ashlyn was very tempted to look. She wasn't sure what the surprise could be, but she was sure it was going to make her moan and cum a lot.

"No peeking," Thalia admonished her.

Somehow Thalia always knew what Ashlyn was thinking. She wriggled around on the pillows a little bit, getting more comfy.

"Okay, you can look now!"

Ashlyn opened her eyes and was beyond shocked at what she saw.

In front of her was a huge, purple cock. Between Thalia's legs.

"By the goddess! What the hell is that?"

"Um, it's a big cock. To you know, fuck you with."

"I know what it is! How the hell did you get it?"

"Oh I went to this sorceress and said, 'Hey sexy magic lady, can you please give me a gigantic cock so I can fuck this super-sweet and sexy Half-Elf?' And she did!"

Ashlyn tried to process what Thalia just told her. And the fact that there was a huge, throbbing, fully erect succubus cock right in front of her.

"What?!"

Thalia ran her supple fingers through Ashlyn's hair.

"I wanted to be able to pleasure you in all ways possible. I know you like big cocks just as much as juicy pussies. And I'd thought it'd be fun."

Ashlyn wasn't sure what to say.

"So... you did this for me?"

"Yup!"

It was the strangest gift Ashlyn had ever received.

"Oh. That's... um, really sweet."

"Oh good. I'm so glad you like it! Now let's see what I can do with this thing. I've been so excited to fill your super-tight pussy with it."

As the cock twitched in front of her, Ashlyn was getting

pretty excited about it filling her too.

Thalia swung her massive member around, making it spin and bob up and down.

"Wow, these things are so weird."

Ashlyn laughed at how ridiculous the dancing cock looked. Though also how appealing.

"By Zirena, would you stop playing with yourself and just fuck me already."

"Your wish is my command milady."

Thalia flitted behind Ashlyn and kneaded her hands into the soft flesh of Ashlyn's ass.

She let her pulsating shaft slap against Ashlyn's appealing posterior. Then used her cock to spank the Half-Elf a few more times.

Ashlyn squirmed, getting really turned on and needing Thalia's new appendage inside her.

"Thalia, stop teasing me!"

She felt the succubus's marvelous hands on her ass, which was evidently her favorite feature of Ashlyn's body.

"Hey, you promised I could do whatever I wanted to you. So be a good little whore and enjoy your spankings."

Ashlyn squirmed as Thalia delivered another sexy slap. This time with her tail.

"Uhh! Okay, please give me more spankings like the little slut that I am."

"With pleasure!"

Thalia took great delight in spanking Ashlyn with her hands, tail, and cock.

Ashlyn whimpered as her pussy moistened and began to wet the pillows underneath her.

"You have no idea how much fun I'm having," Thalia cooed behind her.

"Oh, I have some idea," Ashlyn groaned as she received

the hardest spank yet.

She felt Thalia run her fingers sensually along her back and her very erect cock press against her ass.

"Okay, you've been such a good little submissive demon hunter, I'll give you what you've been craving."

"Thank the gods!"

"Oh wait. What was it again you wanted?"

"Thalia!"

She knew she was going to regret letting Thalia have her way with her. But who was she kidding? She loved it.

"Is it my throbbing, huge cock you want?"

Ashlyn squirmed. "You know I do!"

"I think I need to hear it."

She couldn't see Thalia, but she knew she had a huge, stupid grin on her face. Okay, fine, she'd give her what she wanted.

"I need your gigantic, delicious succubus cock inside my tight Half-Elf pussy and want you to fill me with your cum!"

"Tight pussy filling coming up!"

"You are so freakin' we… uhhhhhhhh!"

Before she could finish her sentence, the huge head of Thalia's penis slid between her lips and slipped all the way into her pussy.

"By all the gods and goddesses!"

Thalia's cock was beyond huge. And it was filling her pussy in ways Ashlyn had never experienced. It was almost too much for Ashlyn to take but not quite. It fit perfectly inside her, taking up every part of Ashlyn's pussy that was available for residence.

"Holy fuck Ashlyn, your pussy is the tightest thing I've ever felt! How do I feel inside you?"

"Oh gods, you're fucking huge! I can barely take you."

"Are you okay sweetie?"

"Yes! Fuck yes! Your cock feels amazing inside me. Never take it out!"

"Wow! This is even better than I thought. Okay, my little sexy slut, get ready for the fucking of your life."

With that, Thalia brought her shaft back, so just the head was left inside, and plunged it all the way back in. Ashlyn gasped into the sheets. Fuck, Thalia was going to own her with this cock.

Thalia set a steady pace, thrusting expertly into Ashlyn's soaked pussy, drawing out sexy pants and moans.

Thalia's penis felt different than normal ones. It would pulse and vibrate when it was inside Ashlyn, stimulating every inch of her pussy walls and making her scream in ecstasy.

"Oh fuck! Thalia, you're... ohhhhhh!"

Thalia grabbed her bound hands with one hand and her auburn hair with the other, yanking her head off the bed and ramming her harder.

"Oh yes! Yes! Yes!" Thalia yelled. "Ashlyn I love your pussy more than anything in the universe."

Between blissful moans, Ashlyn thought how nice it was to have someone think she had the most amazing pussy in the universe. A pussy she was very happy she had completely given over to her succubus companion.

Thalia slipped her tail into Ashlyn's ass, causing the Half-Elf's body to tense up and shake.

"Uhhhhhhh," she groaned at having both her tight holes plundered.

Thalia pulled her hair a little more, just enough to show Ashlyn how submissive she needed to be without hurting her.

"You like being fucked in both holes, don't you?"

"Fuck yes!"

"Do you want more?

"Gods yes! Fuck me until I cum like your perfect, little

slut."

"Oh sweetie, I love it so much when you talk dirty."

She rammed Ashlyn's tender pussy and ass with the speed only a demon could muster.

Ashlyn shrieked and moaned so loudly and constantly she couldn't get any words out. All she knew was Thalia was consuming her sexually, and she never wanted her to stop.

Thalia reached a hand underneath Ashlyn and found her clit, squeezing it in perfect timing with the overwhelming thrusts of her cock and tail.

"Oh Thalia, I... I'm going to... ahhhhhhh!"

Her body shook so violently she lost all control of it. As she came more powerfully than the hundred other times she had today.

She felt her human-elf cum squirt out around the succubus's huge cock and splatter Thalia's sexy stomach.

And then she felt her demon lover's bulbous shaft seize up and expand. And unload the largest amount of cum Ashlyn ever had shot inside her.

Thalia screamed as she spurted more and more of her sexy succubus sauce into Ashlyn's horny hole. And she set off even more of an orgasmic overload inside the Half-Elf.

After both women squirted out a lot more of their juices, Thalia finally collapsed on top of Ashlyn, untying her arms and taking the pillows out from underneath her and positioning them under Ashlyn's head. Ashlyn could feel some of Thalia's cum, mixed with her own girl juices, spill out of her.

They lay there for a long time. Both of them breathing so hard they couldn't speak.

"Oh my... I can't... Wow," Ashlyn finally managed to get out.

"You can say that again," Thalia agreed. "Your pussy is... wow!"

Ashlyn blushed. "Well so is your cock. I can't believe how much cum you shot into me."

"Oh you should talk Miss 'I can't stop squirting.'"

Ashlyn blushed more. "Hey I'm just trying to live up to being your super-slut."

"You're doing an excellent job!"

Thalia kissed her cute Half-Elf ear.

"But you know we're not done, right?"

Ashlyn sighed. "You're going to make me be your slut all night long, aren't you?"

"Yup! Isn't it great?"

It was funny. Yesterday, Ashlyn never could have imagined thinking it was great. But now, there was nothing she'd rather do.

"Yeah, okay. Just... can we take some breaks so I don't get too sore?"

She knew that huge cock inside her constantly was going to be taxing.

"Of course sweetie! We'll take lots of breaks for smooching and cuddling."

They spent the rest of the day and night making love. Thalia tied her up in lots of different positions, some Ashlyn never could have dreamed up.

They fucked in every way imaginable. And came so many times Ashlyn lost count.

During a break, Talia lay behind her, stroking Ashlyn's hair and cuddling her fondly.

"Um, I... want to ask you something," Thalia said hesitantly.

"Let me guess. You have another super-fun way to tie me up and treat me like an elf slut."

"No, well, yes I do have lots of other ways to do that, but that's not what I wanted to ask you."

Ashlyn turned onto her back, and Thalia positioned her body over her in a perfectly sensual and tender way. She gazed up at her succubus lover.

"Okay, what is it?"

Thalia bit her lip, looking worried. Ashlyn had never seen her this hesitant to say something. She usually just blurted out whatever ridiculously sexual thing was on her mind.

"Thalia, would you just tell me!"

"Okay! I want to drain some of your sexual energy."

"What?!"

"Just a little. It won't hurt you. But it's... what I need to survive."

Of course. Succubi needed to feed off people's sexual shenanigans like Ashlyn needed food and water.

"Oh. So you've been wanting to this whole time we've been together?"

"Um, yes. You have no idea how much willpower it's taken to resist tasting your sweet sexual power."

"Why haven't you?"

"I... wanted to get to know you first. And make sure you were okay with it."

Ashlyn stared at her. Thalia was definitely one unique succubus. Who it seemed was developing feelings for her. Did she feel the same way? Shit.

"Okay."

"Okay?"

"Yeah, you can suck some of my energy. But just a little."

Thalia clasped her tightly. "You're the best demon hunter ever!"

More like the worst, Ashlyn thought. What demon hunter let a sexy succubus tie her up and fuck her a million times. And wanted her to keep doing it.

Thalia moved fully on top of her and held her face gently.

"Just relax and give yourself over to me. It'll feel really good."

Ashlyn couldn't believe it, but she was totally okay trusting her. She lay her arms above her head and presented her body to Thalia.

She felt Thalia's tail enter her pussy and fill her wonderfully. Then felt Thalia's soft lips on hers. But it wasn't like the other kisses. She could feel herself become one with Thalia. It was like part of her was being sucked out and was merging into the demon.

It felt amazing. It was like her body and Thalia's had coalesced into one. Like Thalia was inside every part of her in the warmest, most comfortable, and most pleasurable way possible.

She had the notion of some of her essence leaving her mouth and entering Thalia's as the feeling of utter bliss and oneness consumed Ashlyn. She had never experienced anything like it. It wasn't exactly like sex, but somehow, it was even better. It just felt right. She now realized why no one could resist a succubus once they were in the demon's embrace.

When she regained her senses, she had no idea how much time had passed. She felt lightheaded and fatigued. But other than that, she seemed to be okay.

She saw Thalia lying on top of her, the most euphoric expression Ashlyn had ever seen on her face.

The succubus finally came down from her high and gazed at her.

"Wow. I've never tasted someone as amazing as you. Ashlyn, you're incredible."

Ashlyn had never gotten a compliment quite like that before. Apparently, her inner sexual energy was the tastiest thing ever to succubi.

"Oh. Um, thanks. I... I've never experienced anything like

that. I didn't know it was possible to feel that complete with someone."

Thalia brushed her hair back and massaged her pointed ear.

"And I only took a little bit. Imagine what it will be like next time when I take more. If... you're okay with that. I promise I won't ever take more than you can handle."

Next time? Did Ashlyn want a next time? Yup. Definitely.

"Well, you do have to eat. So, um, sure I guess I can be your succubus snack."

Thalia gave her a very wet kiss on the cheek. "And a super-tasty one you are!"

"Great to hear. Can we go to sleep now? You've kind of worn me out."

"Mission accomplished! And yes, come here you sexy demon hunter."

Thalia lay on her back and draped Ashlyn over her. She snuggled her face into the succubus's neck.

Thalia wrapped her arms and tail around her. Ashlyn felt a familiar sensation.

"Thalia, your tail's in my ass."

"Yeah, where else would it be?"

Ashlyn rolled her eyes. Oh boy.

"Well, can you just…"

She felt Thalia adjust it inside her."

"Better?"

"Yeah, oh, that… feels nice."

"Great! Now go to sleep you little anal slut."

"Thalia!"

"I'm kidding! Hey can I help it if I'm obsessed with your luscious ass?"

"You like it that much, huh?"

"I'm in love with your ass."

"You are the weirdest succubus I've ever met."
"Thank you!"
Ashlyn sighed and nestled even closer.
"Goodnight."
"Night sexy ass."

Ashlyn was going to retort but just smiled. She couldn't believe it, but she had become really smitten with the scandalous succubus.

She let herself melt into Thalia's arms, legs, and tail and fell fast asleep.

*****

Ashlyn felt like she was in an earthquake.
"Ashlyn! Wake up, wake up, wake up!"
She opened her eyes and realized it wasn't an earthquake. It was just a nutty succubus shaking her like crazy.
"I'm up, I'm up! What's the matter?"
"I have a dick!"
Ashlyn fell back onto the warm, feathery pillow.
"No kidding. You fucked me with it like a million times last night."
"No I mean I still have it."
"So?"
"So I was supposed to be able to change it back to my delicious pussy anytime I want. But I can't."
Ashlyn sat up. "Wait, you mean…"
"I'm stuck with this huge cock!"
"What?! How… Why… What?!"
"That stupid sorceress must have tricked me. What an evil thing to do!"
"Um, you do know you do mischievous stuff all the time, right?"

"That's different. It's fun when I do it!"

"Sure. Okay, well, there must be a way to fix it."

"Oh great idea! We'll go to that sneaky sorceress and you can kick her ass if she doesn't return my pleasurable pussy."

"Me? How did I get roped into this?"

"Well, I did use a lot of rope on you last night."

Ashlyn shoved her for the terrible joke.

"Listen you're a demon hunter. It's right up your alley."

"A sorceress isn't a demon."

"Close enough."

"And they're not to be trifled with."

"I believe in you. You can do anything!"

She gazed at Ashlyn with her lovely, violet eyes.

"C'mon, please."

How did Ashlyn let herself get into these situations? She knew she was going to regret it, but she couldn't say no to Thalia.

"Ugh, fine."

Thalia flung her arms around Ashlyn.

"You're so cute when you pretend you don't like me."

She kissed Ashlyn on the nose, cheek, neck, and lips.

"Okay, okay, I already said yes."

"What? You don't want me to keep kissing you?"

"No, I do."

"Then shut up and give me those pouty lips of yours."

"My lips are not pou-"

She was cut off as Thalia's tasty tongue was already inside her.

After a bunch of sweet smooching, Thalia clutched her tightly again, pressing Ashlyn's face into her very impressive chest.

"This is going to be a such a fun adventure!"

Ashlyn sighed. "What am I going to do with you?"

"Um, let me fuck you all day and night?"

Ashlyn smiled. That sounded about right.

Thalia wrapped her tail around Ashlyn's waist and pulled her into one last sensual kiss.

This was the strangest friendship Ashlyn had ever had. And definitely the most interesting.

Well, guess they had a sorceress to hunt.

CHAPTER FIVE

Ashlyn leaned over the roof of the house, peering the four stories below her. It was really more like a mansion with how big it was, though not as ostentatious as most nobles' homes. Guess the occupant didn't feel the need to show everyone how rich she was.

Ashlyn felt two soft hands grab her perky butt through her skintight emerald leggings.

"Thalia! Would you cut it out?"

Her succubus friend pouted at her. Friend? Yeah, Ashlyn couldn't deny she had taken to the fiendish demon who was obsessed with sex.

She glanced back and gazed at Thalia's flawless deep purple skin, at her long black locks that cascaded past her bare shoulders, at her two cute horns protruding from her head. And of course, at her incredible breasts that seemed to jiggle provocatively even when she wasn't moving.

Thalia was of course naked, like always. All succubi seemed to have a strong aversion to wearing clothes. Which was very unhelpful when Ashlyn was trying to keep her mind on the mission.

Her idiotic new demon friend had gotten herself in a real pickle. She asked a Sorceress, whose house they were perched on top of, to give her a huge cock, so she could plunder Ashlyn's Half-Elf depths and make her scream and cum all night long. She was extremely successful at that. Ashlyn's cheeks turned rosy at remembering all the ultra-slutty things she cried out in the midst of their seemingly non-stop lovemaking.

But now Thalia couldn't get the cock to revert back to her perfect pussy. So she had recruited Ashlyn to help her convince the Sorceress to do some cock-to-pussy magic.

Ashlyn didn't know how she got roped into these things.

"What?" her purple friend replied to Ashlyn. "You mean you don't want me to do this?"

She squeezed Ashlyn's firm ass hard, making Ashlyn squeal sensually.

"No, I... ohhhh, okay fine."

She was trying to say no, but the way Thalia was kneading her flesh, it was proving extremely difficult.

Ashlyn lay out on her stomach, surveying the house and surroundings.

Thalia climbed on top of her and ran her long, sinuous tongue into the grooves of Ashlyn's pronounced elf ears while grinding her rock hard cock between her lover's ass cheeks.

"Thalia, I... oh goddess... can't concentrate when you're... ohhhh... doing that."

Her elf ears were extremely sensitive and Thalia knew all the best places to explore. And her leggings were so tight that Thalia's magic dick was sliding between Ashlyn's hot cheeks with no problem.

"Oh c'mon sweetness," the succubus cooed into her ear. "You know I can't resist your luscious body."

Ashlyn appreciated the compliment. And appreciated even more how deep Thalia's tongue was inside her ear. She squirmed underneath her demon lover's expert touch.

But she knew if they didn't stop, they'd succumb to non-stop hot demon-elf sex and would never complete their mission.

"Thalia!" she scolded her unusual friend. "We need to get inside and find the Sorceress. You can do all the wicked things you want to me later."

Thalia squeezed Ashlyn tightly. "Promise?"

Ashlyn sighed. "Yes I promise."

She wasn't sure why she kept pretending she had to be talked into it. She loved every single way Thalia made her a submissive little Half-Elf slut. But she did have a reputation to uphold as a fearsome demon hunter. So figured she should at least put up the pretense of not enjoying it.

"Okay deal!" Thalia would go along with pretty much anything as long as Ashlyn promised to give her sensual and firm body over to the demon afterward. "What's the plan my sexy demon hunter?"

"There's a balcony below us but it's a ways down."

Thalia peeked over her shoulder, her large, perfectly firm breasts moving wonderfully along Ashlyn's back.

"Oh no problem."

She flipped over Ashlyn and hung down from the ledge of the roof. "Climb down me and use my tail to swing to the balcony."

Ashlyn felt like there was a reason she should protest this plan, but she couldn't think of one. At least not when it involved clambering all over the demon's curvy, naked body.

She reversed her position and slid down the succubus's back. She placed her right foot against the side of the house, but a brick gave away, and she felt herself start to plummet. She grabbed onto the closest things she could. Which were Thalia's two tremendous orbs. She squeezed Thalia's tits fiercely, hanging on for dear life.

"Ohhhhhh by Zirena! Yes Ashlyn, squeeze my demon tits!"

Ashlyn rolled her eyes. She wasn't even trying to turn Thalia on, but somehow still managed to do it. She also marveled at just how phenomenal her lover's breasts were. They were so large and perfectly firm, they were easily providing excellent handholds for Ashlyn.

She got her footing back and scooted down to Thalia's waist. She grabbed Thalia's long, sinuous tail around the base, where it was thickest. She worked her way hand over hand down the sexy tendril.

"Ohhh yes! Stroke it you Half-Elf slut! Jerk off my tail and make me cum!"

"Thalia!" The horny demon was going to alert the Sorceress and the whole town they were there if she didn't shut up.

She kept lowering herself, wondering why succubus tails had to be so damn sensitive. Every time she touched it, Thalia got incredibly turned on.

The evidence of that hit Ashlyn right in her face. Some of Thalia's sultry sauce dripped out of her pussy and onto Ashlyn's cheek, nose, and lips. She ran her tongue along them and tasted the sweetest sauce in the world. She loved licking up Thalia's demon juice, and the more she did, the hornier she got.

As she opened her mouth to receive more of her new lover's gift, she felt the slick juices run down Thalia's tail.

Oh Shadses. Not again.

She grasped at the wet tail but couldn't get a firm grip. She slipped off it and cursed as she plummeted.

She landed on the balcony with a groan. She looked up and got a another splattering of demon cum on her face. Stupid sexy, super-tasty succubus.

She wiped some of the cum off her cheek and sucked it off

her finger as she sat up. Goddess, she really wanted to go down on Thalia now.

It hadn't been too far of a drop so she was none the worse for wear except maybe a bruise or two.

She saw the doors to the balcony were open. The breeze billowed out the white curtains, and through them she saw one of the most spectacular sights of her life.

A gorgeous woman emerged from a wooden tub of water, arching her back and tossing her long dark brown hair behind her. The setting sun caught the multitude of droplets flinging back from the womans hair, creating a wet, rose-colored kaleidoscope.

The woman's nude body was bathed in golden and pink colors, and as she rose from the tub, Ashlyn could see her magical curves, starting with her supple breasts, across her shapely hips, and down her long, sensual legs.

She was beyond beautiful. And the fact that she was glistening with tiny droplets all over her just enhanced the appeal.

Ashlyn was frozen in place. Watching the woman through the undulating curtains, her mouth hanging open.

Shadses. Why did Sorceresses always have to be so freaking hot?

As the Sorceress turned and Ashlyn's breath caught at getting to see a smooth and perfectly rounded magic ass, she heard what sounded like a yell above her.

She glanced up and a sexy, purple body fell right on top of her.

She groaned much louder this time, lying on her back with Thalia's ultra-sensual nude form right on top of her, the succubus's face right inbetween Ashlyn's breasts.

"Thalia! What the hell?" she yell-whispered.

"Sorry. I slipped."

"Are you going to get off me?"

"I'm good here."

She still had her beautiful face where it was, right at home between the Half-Elf's perky twin assets.

Ashlyn was about to shove her off, when the curtains parted as if by magic.

"Well, well, what do we have here?" a melodious and sensual voice asked.

Ashlyn and Thalia looked up and saw the Sorceress standing over them, wearing a sheer robe that was barely covering any of her breasts and which was left open to leave her pussy completely on display.

Oh Zirena. So much for being stealthy.

CHAPTER SIX

She was so much more beautiful close up. And her pussy was perfect. It was right there, hovering over both women, almost seeming to throb with desire. Ashlyn couldn't take her eyes off it. She had a feeling Thalia couldn't either. In fact she knew she couldn't because she could feel the succubus's cock grow incredibly hard and rub against her pussy, which in turn made Ashlyn moist.

"Oh hey sexy sorceress lady," Thalia greeted her as she shifted on top of Ashlyn and her large erect nipples brushed across Ashlyn's, sending sparks through her whole body. "I'm back."

The Sorceress ran her hand down her wet thigh and did nothing to try to cover up. "I can see that. And I see you brought a lovely friend."

She took in Ashlyn's body with a rather imperceptible look. Though Ashlyn had a feeling the Sorceress was imagining all the naughty things she wanted to do to her.

Ashlyn waved awkwardly. "Um, hi."

The Sorceress smirked and twirled around, her robe swirling in ways that highlighted the most intimate parts of her. "Come. Let's talk inside."

Ashlyn and Thalia scrambled to their feet. As they

followed the Sorceress inside, Ashlyn shoved her demon friend.

"Hey! What's that for?" the succubus complained.

"For falling on top of me. We were supposed to be making a stealthy entrance."

"Well excuse me. Perhaps if a certain Half-Elf slut wasn't jerking off my tail so hard I wouldn't have had such a hard time hanging on."

"I was not jerking you off, you little-"

Ashlyn stopped mid-sentence as Thalia's lips pressed against hers. A warm sensation spread from her mouth through her entire body, as if her entire insides were glowing.

She gasped as Thalia pulled away, her lips trying to cling to the succubus's and never let go.

"You're so cute when you pretend to be mad."

Ashlyn hated it when Thalia did that. Every time she got annoyed at the flirty creature, Thalia would kiss her, or say something charming, or embrace her lovingly. Okay, maybe she didn't totally hate it.

As she looked back ahead, she thought she saw the Sorceress's robe turn translucent for a moment. In that fleeting moment, she saw one of the most wondrous backsides in the five lands. It rivaled Thalia's for perfection. Though the demon's was still her all-time favorite posterior.

Ashlyn was so enamored of the magical ass before her that she almost didn't notice her surroundings. They were in the Sorceress's bedroom. There was a beautiful, ornate four-poster bed to their left. It was purple and gold and had a lovely canopy covering it. On the right side was an intricately carved oak rocking chair and similarly carved wooden chest, designed with dragons on its top. The walls were framed with various paintings of nature done in lovely pastels.

Ashlyn was impressed. It was definitely one of the nicest

bedrooms she had ever been in.

The Sorceress pushed her robe off her shoulders and let it fall. Her ass was revealed in all its magical glory, perfectly perky and supple.

The robe stopped just before it hit the floor, floating in mid-air. She flung her hand to the right, and the robe whisked off into her closet, which opened automatically.

She spun around and waved both hands toward her. Several towels flew out of the closet and began drying off every inch of her sultry body.

Ashlyn and Thalia stood dumbstruck, entranced by the ways the soft, white towels were moving between the Sorceress's legs and making her breasts jiggle spectacularly.

"I love magic," Thalia murmured.

Ashlyn elbowed her to shut up, though she couldn't disagree with her seductive friend's assessment.

The Sorceress glanced at them. Then waved her hand.

And all of Ashlyn's clothes were ripped off. Leaving her standing completely naked.

"Ahhh!" she cried in shock, trying to cover up her naughty bits. "What the hell?!"

"Come now," the Sorceress said as she raised her arms to give the towels better access. "It just wasn't fair that you were the only one clothed. Or that you were hiding your delightful Half-Elf gifts from us."

"I knew I liked her!" Thalia proclaimed.

Ashlyn whacked her in the shoulder. "You're not helping!"

"I'm helping a lot. I'm agreeing you should always be naked. Now show the lady those fantastic tits and pussy."

Ashlyn was going to protest but she caught the devilish look on both Thalia and the Sorceress's faces. And realized how eager they were to see her womanly virtues.

She sighed and moved her hands, showing off her firm,

perky tits and adorable pussy.

"Mmm," the Sorceress sighed. "Those do not disappoint."

"Oh wait till you see her ass," Thalia exclaimed.

And with that she spun Ashlyn around and spanked her pert butt.

"Ah! Thalia would you knock it off?" Ashlyn's cheeks turned red. Both the ones on her face and her ass.

"C'mon sweetness, it's downright evil not to show everyone your sexy-as-hell ass."

Ashlyn turned around and was about to give Thalia one of her annoyed glares, but the succubus wrapped her tail around her waist and pulled her in close.

"I hate you."

"Aw, thanks sexy ass."

Ashlyn wrinkled her nose at her. Somehow Thalia always took "I hate you" to mean the opposite. The flirty fiend was very intuitive.

"You two are quite adorable," the Sorceress proclaimed, now done being dried but apparently not in a hurry to get dressed. "I assume this is the woman for whom you begged me to give you a huge cock."

"She sure is," Thalia replied, licking her long violet tongue along Ashlyn's ear and making her shudder.

The Sorceress turned her gaze to Ashlyn. "And what is the name of the beautiful Half-Elf who's captured the heart of a demon?"

"Ash... Ashlyn Summersnow." The way the Sorceress was staring at her was throwing her off a little. She didn't trust sorcerers or sorceresses. Some were okay but they too often had their own agendas and would do anything to achieve their goals.

"I've heard of you. You have quite the reputation for being a fearsome demon hunter."

"Oh, well... thanks."

"My name is Cassandra. Have you been enjoying the magical cock I gave your lover?"

Geez, that was a little personal. Especially sine they just met.

"Oh, um... yes, it's nice."

"Nice? Nice?!" Thalia replied in outrage. "That's the understatement of the millennium. You became the biggest whore in the five lands for me when I dominated your sexy Half-Elf cunt with my humongous cock."

"Thalia!!" Ashlyn blushed furiously then tackled her non-tactful friend to the floor.

They wrestled as they shouted at each other.

"You're not supposed to tell everyone about our sex life!"

"Why not? It's... ow, that's my tail... amazing."

"Stop pinching my boob! And a relationship is supposed to be private between the two people, not broadcast to the five lands."

"Well you... wait, are we in a relationship?"

They stopped, Thalia on top of Ashlyn, both their chests heaving, as they gazed into each other's eyes.

"I..." Ashlyn looked into the vibrant violet eyes above her. She actually wasn't sure what she wanted with Thalia. She knew as a demon hunter it was ridiculous to be in a relationship with a succubus. But also knew she really enjoyed being around Thalia and being intimate with her. "I don't know. Maybe."

"Oh." Thalia seemed confused as well. Ashlyn knew she was used to being a purely sexual creature, feeding off one sexy victim and then moving to the next. She probably had never contemplated being in a serious relationship.

"Ladies, while your awkward flirting is quite fascinating, I do have things to attend to. Is there a reason you were trying to sneak into my abode?"

She flicked her fingers and another robe, this one a silky aqua, drifted out of the closet and fitted itself onto her arms and hung down around her curvy hips. She didn't make any effort to close it.

Thalia scooted off Ashlyn and helped her to her feet.

"Yes!" she told Cassandra. "You said I'd be able to change this cock back to my irresistible pussy anytime I wanted. But now I can't get rid of this huge salami."

"I said if everything went well, you'd be able to change back," the Sorceress corrected her. "I also warned you there could be complications. You came to me because I'm one of the few sorceresses whose magic works on demons. But even so, it's unpredictable how it will take. You're fortunate your penis wound up in the right place and not coming out of your very alluring posterior."

"Thalia!" Ashlyn scolded. "Why did you take such a risk when you knew it might not work?"

"Ashlyn, life's dull if you don't take chances. And besides I didn't hear you complaining. What I did hear is you begging for me to fill your tight Half-Elf pussy with my huge-"

"Okay we get it!" Ashlyn cut in before Thalia could reveal even more embarrassing intimate details of how she used her cock to dominate her.

The Sorceress sat on the edge of her bed and leaned back with her arms behind her, still very naked. "Well if you both are enjoying it so much, it seems like it all worked out."

"But I want my cute purple pussy back!" Thalia whined.

Ashlyn looked at her friend's throbbing dick. She felt bad. She certainly had loved what Thalia did to her with it, but she of course wanted her to be returned to her normal state and be happy. And she really missed that purple pussy too.

"Can... can you help her?" she asked the Sorceress

sincerely.

Cassandra considered it. Then sat up. "Yes. But I want something in return. Actually two somethings."

Ashlyn tensed up. Making a deal with a Sorceress was never a good idea. Her eyes narrowed. "What is it?"

"I want you two to fuck each other in front of me and then let me use my magic to make you both my sex toys."

Ashlyn's jaw dropped. That definitely wasn't what she was expecting.

"Hey!" Thalia piped up. "That's my job, turning sluts like Ashlyn into sex toys."

"Hey!!" Ashlyn protested.

The demon hugged her with her tail again. "Sorry sweetness. But I do really love making you my slut."

Ashlyn blushed. She loved it too.

Cassandra tugged her lovely legs up on the bed and tossed her still somewhat damp hair behind her. "That may indeed be your job Thalia. But that's my stipulation. Do you accept?"

Ashlyn and Thalia looked at each other.

"Can me and my favorite Half-Elf slut talk it over?"

Ashlyn rolled her eyes. By Pherena, she was going to kick Thalia's ass after this.

"Of course. Take your time." Cassandra motioned with her hand and a well-read tome floated over to her. She lay back and began to read.

Thalia snatched Ashlyn's hand and pulled her out to the balcony. "Well, what do you think?"

"What do I think? I think you are the craziest, most troublemaking succubus I've ever met and you've gotten us into a ridiculous situation."

"Well, yeah. So are you game for becoming her sexual playthings?"

Ashlyn sighed. "Thalia…"

The demon put a gentle finger to Ashlyn's soft lips. "Ashlyn, I know it's a lot, but will you please help me? I really want my pussy back. It's... kind of everything to me as a succubus." She took Ashlyn's hand and squeezed them. "I'll be your sexy demon friend forever if you help me."

She gave Ashlyn one of her classic mischievous smiles, but Ashlyn could tell there was sincerity and even a little worry behind it.

Ashlyn stepped in close and kissed her. "Of course I'll help you, you little Neeper."

Thalia smiled and wrapped her arms, legs, and tail around her. "I knew I could count on you, my sweet little Half-Elf."

Ashlyn felt lemonflies in her stomach. Thalia was using affectionate names for her instead of calling her a slut. Not that Ashlyn minded being called that when they were in the midst of intense lovemaking. It actually turned her on something fierce. But it was nice to see Thalia begin to show more tender feelings for her.

Thalia flicked her tail along Ashlyn's bottom, tickling it pleasantly. "And besides we get to have lots of kinky sex. So it's pretty much a win-win."

Ashlyn slipped her hand into Thalia's and let the cute demon pull her along. When she put it that way, agreeing to the Sorceress's terms didn't sound so bad.

"Okay," Thalia announced as the reentered the room. "Me and sexy pants, er, no pants, over here are in."

Ashlyn made a face at Thalia and glanced down. Not only was she not wearing any pants, her crotch was getting hotter at being in such close proximity to Thalia's naked demon body while being nude herself. And at the thought of what they were about to do. And what the Sorceress was going to do to them.

Cassandra snapped her book shut and rose gracefully from

the bed. "Wonderful. You may use my bed."

She waved her hand and the rocking chair slid across the room, stopping near the foot of the bed. She deposited her perfect posterior in it and crossed her legs, looking at the naked Half-Elf and demon expectantly.

Ashlyn shivered. She wasn't shy about having kinky sex. She proved that with Thalia over the past couple of days. But she had never done it with someone watching before. That was a little weird. And nervewracking.

Thalia pulled her close and purred into her ear. "Don't worry my sweet, I'll take care of you. Just give yourself over to me."

Ashlyn shuddered for a different reason. She had found it very easy to give herself to Thalia, especially when she let her demon hunter defenses down and allowed Thalia's full succubus seduction powers take hold. She was feeling them strongly right now and wanted Thalia to throw her onto the bed and ravish her.

"I see you enjoy being submissive," the Sorceress informed Ashlyn as she traced her long fingers along her creamy thighs.

Thalia pulled Ashlyn tightly against her. "Let's show her exactly how much."

Ashlyn gazed into her eyes and nodded. The Sorceress just better live up to her end of the bargain.

Thalia wrapped Ashlyn up and brought her purple lips to hers, kissing her deliciously. As her supernatural tongue slid inside Ashlyn's mouth, she pushed gently and they fell onto the bed. It was the perfect blend of firm softness and seemed to meld perfectly to Ashlyn's curves. What was also melding perfectly was Thalia's tongue and Ashlyn's. Ashlyn followed the succubus's lead, trying to match the expert twirling of her friend's ridiculously pliable tongue.

Thalia scooted them up the bed until they were near the

headboard. Ashlyn had the sense Thalia was doing something above her head with her hands, but she was too engrossed in Thalia's sweet kisses and the extreme feelings of desire spreading through her entire body. She knew it was Thalia's innate succubus power at work. She also knew she was letting it wash over her without trying to resist in the least, unlike their first meeting. She couldn't believe it had barely been two days since she had known the sneaky demon and they were already in some kind of weird friendship with submissive benefits.

Ashlyn let Thalia pull her hands over her head, and then she felt something soft wrap around her wrists and bind them to the headboard.

She glanced above her and saw Thalia had taken one of the pillow coverings off and used it to tie her up. The sexy demon was an expert at using her environment to make her partners compliant.

She used more of the soft sheets to tie Ashlyn's legs spread apart to two of the bed posts. Ashlyn tugged on her bonds. Yup, she was nice and snuggly tied up and ready for Thalia to have her way with her.

The succubus slipped her hand underneath the back of Ashlyn's head and slipped a pillow underneath it. Ashlyn smiled at her. That was awfully sweet for a creature who supposedly only lived to have sex.

Thalia rubbed her nose with Ashlyn's and then kissed her. "Ready to be made into the ultimate slut?"

"Oh yes!" Ashlyn replied breathlessly before she even realized the words were out of her mouth.

"Good." Thalia smirked and slowly crawled down the Half-Elf's athletically sensual body. As she did, Ashlyn gazed at the canopy above the bed. It sparkled with constellations of the night sky. It was actually a rather romantic thing to make love under. Ashlyn wondered if the Sorceress always had them up there or did it especially for them.

That thought fled her brain as Thalia's tongue reached her pussy and ran sinfully along her outer lips. Ashlyn gasped loudly and her back arched off the bed.

She heard Cassandra snap her fingers and in an instant she and the chair teleported to the side of the bed. Evidently she wanted a better view of Thalia's expert ministrations to Ashlyn's very wet pussy.

The demon's pliable tongue curled all around Ashlyn's lips, almost penetrating them but not quite. The Half-Elf squirmed in blissful agony.

"Oh Thalia! Please... please slip inside me."

Thalia looked up at her with eager, mischievous eyes. "Are you sure that's what you want?"

"Goddess yes! I want it so badly!"

"Tell me what I want to hear sweetness."

Ashlyn usually pretended to resist that request but at this point Thalia knew her too well.

"By Zirena, turn me into your little Half-Elf slut and make me cum like a fountain!"

"Oh Ashlyn, you never disappoint me." Thalia had the biggest grin on her face. Ashlyn knew it brought immense pleasure to her succubus lover when she admitted how submissive she wanted to be. And the more they made love, the easier it was becoming for Ashlyn to very freely admit it.

Thalia's tongue pierced Ashlyn's saturated lips and made her moan loud and long as the succubus wormed inside her. Thalia's tongue was so much longer than a human or elf's that she easily reached every part of Ashlyn's womanhood, even as far back as her cervix.

Ashlyn writhed on the bed, her whole body inflamed with overwhelming pleasure. As her head whipped from side to side, she noticed the Sorceress inch closer and spread her legs, reaching her fingers toward her pussy. She was evidently really enjoying the sex show Ashlyn and Thalia were putting on for her. Ashlyn was really enjoying it too.

"Make her cum succubus. Long and hard."

Thalia didn't need to be told twice. Her tongue found Ashlyn's ultra-sensitive clit and twirled around it in supernatural ways. She completely wrapped up Ashlyn's clit and tugged on it.

"Ahhhhhhh!" Ashlyn screamed in blissful nirvana. No one could control her nubile nub like Thalia.

Thalia performed her succubus magic on Ashlyn's throbbing clit, making Ashlyn's body buck and thrash uncontrollably. And then she was cumming uncontrollably.

"Oh goddess Thalia I'm cumming! I'm cumming so hard!"

She could feel her Half-Elf juices squirt out of her and into Thalia's mouth. Her demon lover sucked them up like they were the nectar of the gods. Bringing Ashlyn to even greater heights of orgasmic pleasure.

Ashlyn could feel it across her entire body. It was like her orgasms were consuming her from the inside. She felt like this was the only thing she was meant to do: spill her womanly juices for Thalia and never stop.

When the most intense of the orgasms were subsiding and Thalia had drunk up a ridiculous amount of Ashlyn's succulent sauce, the succubus climbed up Ashlyn's bound body and delivered one of the most intense kisses of Ashlyn's life.

As she was being consumed by Thalia's lips, she felt the demon's enormous magical cock slip inside her.

Her huge moan was engulfed by Thalia's mouth as her body seized up and her pussy was filled in the most delicious way possible.

Thalia thrust back and forth, changing speeds and forcefulness, and fucking Ashlyn's tight Half-Elf pussy perfectly.

Ashlyn continued to groan and moan into Thalia's tasty tongue and lovely lips as she was dominated by Thalia's phallus.

She felt a tendril brush her ass and knew it was Thalia's tantalizing tail. The tail lapped up some of Ashlyn's juices dripping out of her engorged pussy and then pierced Ashlyn's extremely tight ass.

"Oh Zirena!" Ashlyn loudly evoked the goddess of love and desire as Thalia briefly released her lips. "Thalia... I..."

She couldn't finish as Thalia attacked her with passionate kisses again as her tail plunged farther into her. Ashlyn loved how it felt inside her. Loved how her ass muscles clamped around Thalia's wonderful tail and hugged it lovingly.

Thalia's tongue was so far into Ashlyn's throat, her tail so far inside her ass, and her cock so deep in her pussy, Ashlyn was getting an overwhelmingly intense fucking in all three holes.

She came again. Just as hard and spectacularly as before. And then she felt Thalia explode inside her and shoot her magical demon sperm into her tight cunt. She moaned and squealed as she was filled with a huge amount of Thalia's seed and expelled an equally huge amount of her own.

When Thalia finally pulled out of her, she somehow still had some sticky sauce left, which she promptly deposited all over Ashlyn's tits and stomach. She then collapsed on top of her Half-Elf lover, peppering her cheek with sweet kisses and stroking her long, auburn hair.

"Thanks... for the present," Ashlyn told her when she was finally able to catch her breath.

"My pleasure sweetness. You should constantly be covered

in my juices."

Ashlyn wrinkled her nose at her but wasn't going to complain. She was enjoying cuddling with Thalia after getting fucked so wonderfully.

She heard a contented sigh, and she and Thalia raised their heads.

They saw the Sorceress leaning back in the chair, her robe off her shoulders and down around her arms, her heaving breasts gleaming, her nipples fully erect, and her legs spread with wetness covering her crotch and thighs. She had obviously really gotten herself off watching Ashlyn and Thalia's kinky sexcapades.

"Ohh, you two were wonderful."

"Well, I am an expert at this kind of stuff," Thalia replied proudly. "And I do have the biggest slut in the five lands as my partner."

"Hey!" Ashlyn protested. She would have whacked her, but her hands were still bound.

The demon kissed her. "That's a compliment."

"Gee, thanks." Ashlyn made a face at her but wasn't really mad. She was getting used to Thalia's sexy teasing.

She turned to the Sorceress. "Okay, so can you give this sex maniac her pussy back?"

Thalia took absolutely no offense at being called a sex maniac. Ashlyn realized it was probably a huge accolade.

Cassandra licked the juices off her fingers. Ashlyn and Thalia both stared at her, watching in rapture. Apparently, the Sorceress liked being plenty kinky too.

"Oh, we're just getting started," she told them. "Now it's my turn to turn your delicious bodies into the sex toys they should be."

Ashlyn shuddered and even felt Thalia shiver a little. What exactly did the Sorceress have in store for them?

The Sorceress's eyes glowed yellow as she rotated her wrists and made intricate patterns in the air with her fingers.

Ashlyn's bonds released her and she and Thalia flipped over, exchanging positions, so Ashlyn was on top of her demon lover. Then she was yanked up to her knees and her arms forced above her. Goddess, Cassandra was a powerful Sorceress. She was completely manipulating Ashlyn's body however she wanted.

She felt invisible threads wrap around her wrists and bind them together. Then lift her upward, so her knees were off the bed.

Thalia must have had the magical bindings encircling her as her arms and legs were pulled to the bed posts and she seemed to be unable to yank them free.

Her body was scooted down the bed, so her huge cock was right underneath Ashlyn's pussy, which was still leaking a little of her own cum and Thalia's.

The Sorceress curled her fingers together and Thalia let out a low, sultry growl as her cock grew and got incredibly hard.

Maybe it was just the angle, but Ashlyn thought it looked bigger than it had moments ago. Her pussy was suspended above Thalia's quivering member, almost touching its bulbous head.

The Sorceress climbed onto the bed and knelt next to them.

"Do you want me to drop you onto her huge cock and make her spear you like a little whore?"

Ashlyn gulped. This Sorceress was rivaling Thalia for being super-kinky.

Cassandra flicked her finger at Thalia, making her arch her back and cry out. "Ohh Ashlyn! I need your pussy so bad!"

Ashlyn could see her friend's purple penis twitching rapidly, obviously needing the sweet release that could only be found in her tiny cavern.

She heard the Sorceress's voice in her ear even though the talented magician hadn't moved. "Come now Ashlyn. If you want me to help your friend, you need to be completely honest about how slutty you love being."

Ashlyn cursed internally. Why did she keep meeting these women who were so adept at making her reveal her submissive desires?

"Okay yes! I want Thalia to fill my super-tight pussy and own it. It completely belongs to her!"

Cassandra smiled. "That's better."

And then the magical bonds released her, and she fell right onto Thalia's shaft. She sunk all the way down to its base, the cock spearing her so deep and hard she almost passed out.

"Oh goddessssssss!!" she screamed as her pussy completely submitted to Thalia's cock and begged it to never leave.

The Sorceress waved her hands, lifting Ashlyn up and dropping her again and again on Thalia's wonderful purple penis.

Ashlyn cried out in a mix of pain and pleasure, though she didn't want the Sorceress to stop. She wanted to take everything her succubus lover had to offer.

Thalia was just as vocal, her sexy moans driving Ashlyn wild with desire. She could feel Thalia's succubus charms spilling out of her, and mixed with the Sorceress's magic, made Ashlyn want to be fucked long and hard and made to spill every ounce of her Half-Elf juices all over Thalia's cock, stomach, and hips.

Her thighs and legs were already covered in her own cum as her body was continually impaled on Thalia like a sex toy. Her tits bounced out of control and she could see Thalia staring at them lustfully.

"Oh Ashlyn, you're the sexiest, most alluring creature I've ever fucked."

Ashlyn would have blushed if she wasn't being fucked out of her mind. Coming from a succubus who must have slept with hundreds if not thousands of people, that was quite the compliment.

"Thalia... I..." she tried to return the amorous accolades but dissolved into blissful cries instead. "Oh gods and goddesses, I'm going to cum!"

Cassandra used her magic to lift her off Thalia and a volcano of Half-Elf cum came pouring out, splattering Thalia's cock, stomach, and legs as well as the bed.

"Ohhhhhhhhhhhhhh!" Ashlyn moaned in orgasmic delight.

She was rammed back down onto Thalia's cock, which had its own eruption, shooting the succubus's sweet and sticky cum up into her very full pussy.

The Sorceress raised her up again, and Thalia's succulent seed sprayed Ashlyn's stomach and thighs, mixing with her own cum that was coming out non-stop.

Back down she went, getting speared by Thalia's delicious cock while magical demon cum was shooting out of it.

By the time they were done, Ashlyn and Thalia were a sweet and sticky mess, their bodies covered in each other's juices. Ashlyn's magical bonds released her and she fell on top of her demon lover, her breasts pressed wonderfully against Thalia's larger mounds, her head resting on the succubus's silky hair that spilled over her shoulders.

She panted heavily. "Oh Thalia... please hold me."

Thalia's invisible bonds also released her and she enveloped Ashlyn with her arms and tail, squeezing her tightly.

"I've got you sweetness." She ran her fingers through Ashlyn's hair and kissed her forehead.

The Sorceress lay on her side next to them, propping her

head up with her hand, the robe just barely covering her.

"Are you both having fun? I sure am."

"You're so evil," Thalia replied. "I'm really impressed."

Ashlyn couldn't help but laugh amid her panting. Of course, Thalia loved seeing kinky wickedness in others.

"But I don't think you've made my favorite Half-Elf enough of a slut yet. She needs to be shown what a total whore she can be."

"Thalia!" Ashlyn complained.

Cassandra dipped her finger in their cum mixture and sucked it off. Goddess this woman was really kinky.

"Mmm, oh I agree. But so do you."

"Yes!" Thalia exclaimed. "Wait, what?"

"I'm going to turn you both into my whores."

"Ha!" Ashlyn teased, loving that Thalia was on the other end of things for a change. She pinched the demon's nipple hard, the way she knew Thalia liked it. "This is going to be so worth it."

"Ashlyn!"

"Yes demon slut?"

Thalia screwed up her cute nose. She hated it when the tables got turned on her. "Hey, I'm a succubus. We do the whoring, I mean whore-making, I mean, oh you know."

The Sorceress was sucking up more of their wicked cum-hybrid. "Do you want your pussy back or not?"

Thalia looked like she was fighting some kind of internal battle over a sacred succubus code.

Ashlyn took her face gently in her hands and kissed her. "Hey, I'll be with you the whole time. It'll be fun to be sluts together."

She couldn't believe she just said that. But she wanted to reassure Thalia. And she was getting turned on thinking about both of them being made to submit together.

"Okay, fine," Thalia gave in. "But I want my perfect pussy back now you wicked witch."

The Sorceress arched her eyebrow, apparently not thrilled about being called a witch.

"It was a compliment," Thalia quickly added. "I love wicked people."

That seemed to satisfy the Sorceress. She motioned for Ashlyn to move. She slid off Thalia so she was laying on her side next to her, still holding her tightly, but allowing the Sorceress access to Thalia's monster cock.

Cassandra scooted onto her knees and held her hands over the magical gift she had bestowed onto the succubus. A yellow-orangish energy emanated from her hands and bathed the immense cock in a magical glow.

"Ahhhhhh!" Thalia yelled as her body seized up.

Ashlyn held her firmly and kissed her, trying to alleviate some of the pain.

After several seconds, the succubus's body relaxed and Ashlyn freed her lips. Thalia looked up at her. And not with lust like she often did, but seemingly with love. But that was ridiculous. Succubi didn't fall in love. Did they?

Ashlyn didn't have time to contemplate that further as Thalia clutched her tightly, like she was trying to squeeze the life out of her.

"Ashlyn! My adorable pussy is back! Look, look, look!"

Ashlyn laughed at her friend's exuberance. "Okay, okay."

She gazed between Thalia's legs and indeed saw the perfectly formed and alluring succubus pussy that she had gotten to know so well yesterday.

"Go kiss it and see how it tastes."

"Thaliaaa."

"C'mon please."

"All right."

It's not like Ashlyn really needed convincing. There was something about a succubus's juices that made them taste like the most delicious substance in the universe. Ashlyn couldn't stop herself from drinking them all up when they got flowing during their lovemaking.

The Sorceress watched them curiously. Apparently okay with letting them have a moment of intimacy before she turned them into her sex toys.

Ashlyn slid down Thalia's curvaceous body and peppered sweet smooches along Thalia's soft and supple lips. They got instantly wet and Ashlyn flicked her tongue out, licking up the sweet succubus juices.

Then she got sprayed in the face as Thalia expelled a nice stream out of her pussy.

"Ah! Thalia!" She should have known her sneaky friend could cum on command like that.

"Open up sweetness."

Ashlyn complied and put her mouth over Thalia's enticing pussy, drinking up everything the demon offered her. It tasted sweet and smelled of lavender and wildflowers and she felt warm and cozy inside after consuming it.

"As you can see, I have given you back your pussy. Now it's time to submit to me in whatever ways I desire."

Thalia brought Ashlyn back up to her lips and kissed her, licking her own juices off the Half Elf's mouth.

"Okay. A deal's a deal."

Ashlyn nodded. "I'm ready."

She was still a little nervous, but with Thalia by her side, she felt safe.

Invisible threads snaked around her body. They encircled her thighs, hips, chest, and arms. They pinned her to Thalia, so their lips were inches apart and their arms and legs were wrapped around each other.

The magic bonds were soft but tightened firmly around them, so they couldn't move. Their tits and pussies were pressed against each other and caused both of them to gasp erotically.

The Sorceress had a big smile on her face as she remained laying next to them. She bent her fingers toward her and back, continually repeating the process.

Ashlyn's hips began to grind against Thalia's, rubbing her already tender pussy against Thalia's newly restored one. Neither of them were trying to do it. The Sorceress's magic ropes were forcing them to pussy fuck each other.

Ashlyn wasn't complaining. It felt wonderful - her clit massaging Thalia's.

"Ohhh, I'm so glad I have my pussy back," Thalia purred.

"Oooo, me too," Ashlyn cooed.

"Kiss each other," the Sorceress commanded.

They were glad to comply. Ashlyn's lips joined Thalia's and she lost herself in the succubus's warm mouth.

The Sorceress's invisible bonds made them fuck harder, smashing their pussies and clits against each other and rubbing them together in extremely sinful ways.

They kissed with more abandon, losing themselves in their magical lovemaking. Ashlyn sucked on Thalia's tongue, drinking in her sweetness. Her saliva tasted just as good as her pussy juices.

The Sorceress let the robe fall down her shoulders again, exposing her bare breasts and hard nipples. She moved her one hand down her stomach until it found its home between her legs, her long fingers penetrating her folds. While she used her other hand to continue conducting the sexual symphony going on next to her.

Ashlyn didn't think she had even been more aroused. She had the most wondrous body she had ever seen fucking her, was making out with Thalia's beautiful mouth, and had a gorgeous naked Sorceress fingering herself right next to them.

Thalia's tail was flicking around like crazy. It did that when she was really horny or in the throes of sexual passion.

"Stick it in your lover's ass," the Sorceress ordered as she now had two fingers deep inside her magical folds.

Thalia's tail lapped up some of their juices then found Ashlyn's tiny hole and explored it extremely thoroughly.

"Oh goddess it's so deep!" Ashlyn groaned as she felt it fill her ass wickedly.

"Are you okay?" the demon asked her between non-stop kissing.

"Y... yes, I... I just feel so slutty."

"Demons, me too! It's so good!"

Ashlyn couldn't disagree. Her body felt like one big erogenous zone that was in a state of perpetual sexual bliss.

Cassandra grinned, loving their admissions of sluttiness. She made them pound their pussies extremely hard. Ashlyn knew she couldn't contain the oncoming onslaught of sexual nirvana.

She moaned loudly into Thalia's eager mouth as she sprayed her sauce all over her friend's clit and lips. A second later Thalia had her release. Letting loose a sultry groan into Ashlyn's mouth as her own juices mixed with Ashlyn's and were wiped all over the Half Elf's pussy.

Thalia's tail kept plundering her ass as the Sorceress's threads didn't give them any rest, making them continue to fuck and spill out as much of their woman and demonhood as possible.

While they were busy doing that, the Sorceress had her own eruption, her magical climax squirting a huge stream of her cum all over Ashlyn and Thalia.

Ashlyn didn't care. She had been coated in so much cum

the past couple of days what was a little more. And she was too engrossed in her non-stop orgasms and Thalia's mouth, which she never stopped kissing.

The invisible bonds slowed down their grinding, letting them come to rest but still holding them together tightly. They whimpered softly as tiny orgasms continue to detonate inside them and the Sorceress continued to give them a bath in her magic sauce.

The Sorceress lay back on the bed, looking very satisfied.

"I must compliment you both. You are wonderful sex toys."

"Um, thanks?" Ashlyn wasn't sure what the correct response was to that.

"Uhh, you are so evil," Thalia added. "Dammit, I really respect your work."

Ashlyn smiled. She knew Thalia wanted to be mad about having the tables turned on her and being forced to be submissive, but she couldn't deny how talented the Sorceress was at a job she took such pride in.

She kissed her lover again. "Don't worry. I'll let you dominate me to your heart's content when we're alone." She figured that would cheer her companion up.

Thalia squeezed her as much as she could within their bonds and kissed her deeply. "Oh you're the best girlfriend ever!"

Girlfriend? Wait, did Thalia just really call her that? A succubus wanted to date Ashlyn and not just fuck her brains out? Ashlyn couldn't get her head around that. Thalia flipped everything she knew about succubi on its head. Of course Ashlyn was the one who had brought up the possibility of a relationship earlier. But she wasn't sure of her own feelings for Thalia. Could she have a real relationship with the most sexual of demons?

Before she could ponder that further, the Sorceress made a

proclamation. "Now it's time to really turn you into submissive playthings."

Ashlyn's eyes went wide. What in Zirena? So what they just did was just a warm-up?

The Sorceress kept her word about completely dominating them.

Magical glowing dildos materialized and fucked their tight pussies and asses mercilessly.

The Sorceress floated them into the air and twisted their bodies into extremely kinky and submissive positions as the magic cocks plundered them and made them scream in pleasure.

At times, Ashlyn was sucking Thalia's sensual tail while being fucked. At others, Thalia was licking Ashlyn's nipples so hard she thought she was going to cum out of her tits.

They were made to lick, suck, and nibble on their clits as the huge cocks filled their caverns. They were fucked upside down, their tits bouncing spectacularly as their spread legs were forced upward to take the Sorceress's monstrous cock creations.

And for the grand finale, Cassandra created a glowing violet cock so large they both took it at the same time, grabbing hold of each other's hips and slamming their drenched pussies onto the double magic dildo until they made contact with each other.

They came so many times Ashlyn didn't think she could possibly have any juices left inside her. At times she felt like she might pass out from an overload of orgasming. But somehow she stayed conscious. And through it all, there was Thalia. Next to her, loving her, gazing at her with those vibrant violet eyes. Eyes she never wanted to stop staring into.

At some point, Ashlyn felt the magic release her and she collapsed on top of Thalia on the bed. And that was the last thing she remembered until sweet sex dreams overtook her.

CHAPTER SEVEN

Ashlyn woke but didn't open her eyes. She felt enveloped in warm and tender limbs and tendrils. She knew it was Thalia's arms, legs, and tail wrapping her up in that way that made her feel completely safe and content.

Her eye's fluttered open and she found her mischievous demon friend staring at her.

"Do you always watch me when I'm sleeping?"

"Yes. You're adorable."

"You're such a weirdo."

"You love it."

"Mm, maybe." She kissed Thalia on the cheek and nestled closer to her.

The demon's tail moved back and forth along Ashlyn's toned butt, massaging it gently.

"Mmm, that feels good."

"Well, I figure you need it after how much I tail fucked your ass last night."

Ashlyn pinched Thalia's sides.

"Ow!"

"Stop teasing me and cuddle you mischievous demon."

"Flattery will get you everywhere," Thalia replied as she ran her fingers along the back of Ashlyn's neck and breathed in her scent.

They lay in silence, Ashlyn riding Thalia's slow breathing, the demon's breasts and body feeling like the warmest, softest and most sensual pillow. This was her favorite part of their sexual shenanigans. Of course, the sex itself was beyond anything she had experienced. But she loved just laying in Thalia's arms and feeling the demon surround her like a loving cocoon. For someone who supposedly was only interested in sex, she was very good at romantic post-coitus cuddling.

Ashlyn would have been content to stay like that forever but a delicious aroma wafted into the room.

Thalia's ears perked up as she sniffed. "Oo, that smells good. That's go have some breakfast! Then post-breakfast sex!"

"You're ridiculous, you know that?"

"Uh huh."

Ashlyn grinned and kissed Thalia on the cheek.

She hopped off the bed and offered Thalia her hand.

The demon accepted it with a smile. "Oh my, how chivalrous. I may swoon."

Ashlyn rolled her eyes. "Can't you be serious about anything?"

"Yup. I can be serious about that amazing Half-Elf ass of yours."

She swatted Ashlyn's perky butt with her tail, making her jump.

Ashlyn shoved her playfully. She was really becoming fond of Thalia spanking her with her lovely tail.

She scanned the room. "Now where did my clothes go?"

"Who cares? You're supposed to stay naked anyway."

"Says who?"

"The Sorceress."

"She did not say that."

"Okay, maybe not. But I'm saying it. So I can ogle your

beautiful body to my heart's content."

Ashlyn tried to cover up her reddening cheeks. "Aren't you getting sick of me?"

Thalia wrapped her tail around Ashlyn's waist and pulled her into a passionate kiss, her hands holding her face tenderly.

"Never sweetness."

She took her hand and yanked her toward the door.

"Now c'mon, whatever's cooking smells even better now."

Ashlyn took a whiff. It did smell good.

She let Thalia lead her along, wondering how a succubus, who generally only visited people once or twice, could want to spend this much time with her.

Maybe Thalia really was falling for Ashlyn. Was she feeling the same way about the annoying, but loveable, demon?

Pherena help her. How did she get herself into these situations?

Oh well. Maybe a full stomach would help her sort things out.

*****

They found the Sorceress in the lavish kitchen downstairs, munching on toasted crestberry bread. She wore one of her favorite short silky robes, this one a pleasant pale blue, and had her legs tucked underneath her on the chair.

"Ah, there you two are. Did you sleep well?"

Thalia pulled Ashlyn close and squeezed her waist. "I always sleep well with this gorgeous creature beside me."

Ashlyn blushed. Geez, Thalia was being awfully amorous. If she kept that up, Ashlyn was probably going to have no choice but to fall for her.

"Excellent. Come, have some breakfast."

Thalia's eyes lit up and she snatched Ashlyn's hand,

yanking her to the table. Even though the succubus didn't need to eat, Ashlyn had discovered she greatly enjoyed it. Ashlyn had always been a big fan of food too. When she was growing up, her mother always joked that she had the appetite of an orc rather than an elf or human.

The Sorceress used her magic to float bread, fruit, and fluffy flatcakes covered with butter over to them. Ashlyn and Thalia dug in hungrily. They had really worked up an appetite with all that submissive sex.

Thalia scooted next to Ashlyn on the wooden bench, so their naked thighs touched as they ate. Ashlyn gulped down a big bite of flatcake and then smiled at her. Oh Pherena, she was starting to seriously consider what it would be like to be Thalia's girlfriend. She couldn't believe she was becoming this smitten with a demon. Well, maybe she could. Even though Thalia could drive her crazy and was obsessed with sex, she was ridiculously fun and and made Ashlyn feel good about herself. And she was surprisingly sweet and caring.

"What?" the lovely demon asked with her mouth full.

"Nothing," Ashlyn replied with a grin. "Don't eat with your mouth full."

"Sorry," Thalia said, her mouth still full.

The Sorceress thought they were adorable and wanted to know how they had met. So they told her the tale, Ashlyn correcting Thalia's ridiculous embellishments.

The Sorceress seemed genuinely entertained by the retelling of their adventures, and they were genuinely happy to have eaten such a delicious meal. Though Thalia was still hungry. But in a different way.

She squeezed Ashlyn's thigh. "Sweetness, is it okay if I..."

Ashlyn knew what she wanted. Succubi needed to regularly feed off people's sexual energy in order to survive. If too much was taken, it could leave the person lifeless. But

Ashlyn trusted Thalia. She knew she'd only take what she needed. Plus the feeling was like heaven. Actually, whatever was beyond heaven.

She patted the hand that was on her thigh. "Yes. It's totally okay."

Thalia's eyes lit up and she straddled Ashlyn, sitting on her lap and tossing her arms around her neck.

"Just relax love."

Ashlyn nodded and relaxed her muscles as she let Thalia pull her into a kiss of epic proportions. She lost all sense of time and space as she felt her essence flow out of her and into Thalia. And felt Thalia's enter her. It was like they were one purely sexual being, their bodies merging in perfect harmony.

Ashlyn felt like there was no one else in the world except Thalia. She was her everything. She consumed her. She was enraptured by her.

She never knew how long Thalia fed on her. It felt like both an instant and eternity. When her lover pulled back, Ashlyn gasped blissfully and collapsed against Thalia's chest.

Thalia held her tightly and rubbed her back as she closed her eyes and melted into her friend's warmth. It always took her a little while to recover from these energy draining sessions.

"Fascinating," she thought she heard the Sorceress comment. "I've never seen a succubus feed up close. I didn't realize it was so tender."

Ashlyn realized it was tender. And even more so than the first time Thalia had fed on her. The succubus was definitely sweet on her.

"It's... not usually," Thalia admitted. "She's special."

Ashlyn hoped she had heard that correctly and it wasn't her imagination from her post-energy sex craze. Because it was one of the sweetest things anyone had ever said about her.

After she got her bearings back, Ashlyn switched positions with Thalia, so she was sitting sideways on the succubus's lap, very content to let her lover stroke her sensitive elf ears and run her fingers through her thick hair.

"Thanks for letting me snack on you sweetness. You taste soooooo good."

"Anytime," Ashlyn replied, kissing Thalia's lovely neck. "You're pretty damn amazing."

"You got that right!"

Ashlyn giggled. Okay, maybe modesty wasn't one of Thalia's strong points, but she had a lot of other loveable qualities.

The Sorceress cleared her throat. "As cute as you two are, it's time to help me with the other thing I require of you."

Ashlyn's eyes snapped open. Shadses. She had forgotten the wily magician had said there were two requirements they had to fulfill in order to restore Thalia's pussy. After last night's marathon slut session, Ashlyn was a little worried about what it would entail. Well, whatever it was, it was worth it to help Thalia. Ashlyn had definitely liked Thalia's cock. But she loved her pussy. And was very glad she now had it back.

Thalia continued to stroke Ashlyn gently as she turned her gaze to Cassandra. "Okay, kinky Sorceress lady, what do we have to do?"

Cassandra hesitated. For the first time since they had met her, Ashlyn saw doubt and insecurity on her face. Now she was really intrigued about what the request would be.

"I... I need your help... winning someone's heart."

Ashlyn gaped at her. "Um, what?"

Thalia squeezed Ashlyn excitedly. "Oo, this just got so much more interesting. Who is it?"

"Her... her name's Kiosa. She's a Corvarean."

Ashlyn's ears perked up. She had met a couple of

Corvareans in her travels. They were known for being the fiercest warriors in the five lands and kept their bodies in peak physical condition. But they were just as known for having highly educated scholars. Warrior poets so to speak.

They were also the only race Ashlyn knew of who didn't grow genitalia until puberty. Each Corvarean decided what sex they wanted to identity with, or sometimes a mixture of sexes or neither sex, and grew the appropriate sex organs. Ashlyn had heard they could also change this choice later in life. Honestly, she didn't really know a lot about their culture, and was eager to learn more.

"Oh hells yes!" Thalia replied excitedly. "I've done things with Corvareans that shouldn't even be legal for demons."

Ashlyn blushed, a little embarrassed she was trying to imagine what was too risque for even Thalia to talk about. She also got a little jealous. She knew Thalia had been with countless partners. But part of her wanted the succubus all to herself. Apparently, a big part of her if she was getting this jealous about it.

Thalia must have noticed, because she hugged Ashlyn fiercely and kissed her sweetly. "Oh, I'm sorry sweetness. Don't worry, you're my all time favorite slut in the whole world. And the only one I want to do super-naughty things with."

Ashlyn managed to smile. For a succubus, she knew that was an incredibly sweet thing to say.

She smooched Thalia, then turned her attention back to Cassandra. "So how do you know Kiosa?"

"Yes tell us everything!" Thalia was apparently fascinated by the Sorceress's crush. Ashlyn didn't realize the demon liked romantic stuff so much. Though maybe she was excited that it would lead to hot sex if they managed to hook the two up.

"I… I've seen her several times when I go into town for

supplies. She works as a sword-for-hire."

"Have you talked to her?" Ashlyn asked.

"Well, not exactly."

"What does that mean?"

"We've exchanged meaningful glances."

"Meaningful glances?" Thalia exclaimed in exasperation. "Just grab her and fuck her!"

"Thalia!" Ashlyn scolded.

Cassandra blushed. Ashlyn was seeing the Sorceress in a totally different light. It was funny how confident and dominant she was last night. And how worried and insecure she was right now. Guess the powerful magician was just like a normal person after all.

Thalia's eyes lit up as she studied Cassandra. "Ohh, I see now."

"See what?" Ashlyn asked. The succubus had the ability to sense what kind of kinky sex people wanted just by being in their vicinity and breathing in their sexual essence.

"She wants Kiosa to grab and fuck her. She wants the sexy Corvarean to make her a submissive Sorceress slut."

Ashyln's eyes widened. She would not have guessed that based on how much Cassandra had dominated them last night. But it was extremely hot. She couldn't help but picture a buff, sexy Corvarean woman tying the Sorceress up and making her submit in the kinkiest ways imaginable.

"I... I do not!" Cassandra protested.

"You can't fool a succubus when it comes to kinky sex honey."

"Yeah, she's kind of got you, you magical slut," Ashlyn added.

"Hey!" Cassandra protested even more.

Whoops. Ashlyn surprised herself by saying that. Thalia must be rubbing off on her.

"Oh, um, sorry. I'm just getting you back for all the slutty stuff you made us scream last night."

Thalia beamed at her. "I am such an excellent influence on you."

Ashlyn stuck her tongue out at her. She wasn't so sure about that, but it was kind of fun to tease Cassandra.

"Listen, are you two going to help me or not?"

The Sorceress crossed her arms petulantly. Ashlyn felt bad for her. She was obviously crushing hard on Kiosa.

"Of course we'll help you," Thalia reassured her.

Ashlyn nodded.

"As long as we get to watch you two have wild, submissive sex after we get you together."

"Thalia!" Ashlyn couldn't believe how naughty her partner was. Okay who was she kidding? She could absolutely believe it.

"What? I know you want to watch just as much as I do."

Ashlyn bit her lip. Okay, she really couldn't deny that she was getting really turned on at the idea of her and Thalia getting to watch the Sorceress be dominated and made to cum. And then the two of them having wild, passionate sex next to them. Geez, when did she get so kinky?

Cassandra stamped her foot. "Okay, fine, you can watch. Just please help me."

Ashlyn slid off Thalia's cozy lap and hopped onto the table, sitting her cute bottom on it to move closer to Cassandra. Thalia scooted her sensual butt and tail next to her.

"Why don't you just, you know, talk to her and ask her out?" Ashlyn asked, stating the obvious.

"I... I can't do that."

"Why not?"

"She's too beautiful and amazing."

Ashlyn took in Cassandra's epic loveliness again. "Um,

you do realize you're one of the most beautiful women in the entire five lands, right?"

From her reaction, she definitely didn't realize that.

"Ashlyn's right," Thalia agreed. "If I wasn't so enchanted with this Half-Elf cutie, I'd be sucking up your sexy Sorceress essence all night long."

She nudged Ashlyn with her thigh. Ashlyn smiled. She was flattered Thalia liked her more than the Sorceress, who was ridiculously gorgeous.

"Oh, well, thank you. But I'm still too nervous to talk to her."

"Okay, I'll use my succubus wiles on her and she'll want to fuck your brains out till you can't take it anymore."

"Thalia, she wants a real relationship with her, not just wild sex."

"Oh." The succubus seemed a little confused by that.

"What if you write her a love poem?"

"Boring!" Thalia decreed. "Who wants to get some sappy old love poem?"

"I do!" Ashlyn retorted.

"Oh, really?"

"Well, yeah. I think it's sweet."

"Oh, okay. Here you go!"

You're a fierce demon hunter, you're really tough
I love seeing you in the buff
Your eyes are so beautiful, you're such a cutie
I love sticking my tail in your luscious booty!

Ashlyn stared at her. Not sure whether to laugh or be touched by Thalia's impromptu ode to her naked butt.

"How was that?"

Ashlyn pecked her on the cheek. "It needs some work, but

I appreciate the effort."

"I am not writing a poem about Kiosa's booty."

Thalia stuck her tongue out at Ashlyn and Cassandra. "You guys just can't appreciate good poetry."

Ashlyn hopped off the table. "Okay, let's head into town and see if she's there. Maybe seeing her will give us some new ideas."

"Very well." Cassandra waved her hand and the dishes and cups floated off the table and deposited themselves in the large sink.

"Oh, and… thank you for helping me."

"No problem," Ashlyn replied. "Apparently, I have a penchant for making friends with women who dominate me in the bedroom."

Thalia hugged her from behind. "Oh yes! You're very good at that."

Ashlyn shook her head, but was secretly happy she had met both Thalia and Cassandra.

"Okay, let's go get you a date!"

CHAPTER EIGHT

They traveled the short distance into the town of Crystal Lake, which had a quaint section of shops on the main thoroughfare the Sorceress took them through.

Cassandra had found Ashlyn's clothes, so she was finally now dressed again. She felt she had been spending way more time naked than clothed the past few days. Not that that was necessarily a bad thing.

Thalia fiddled with her outfit, tugging and pulling on it like it was chafing her everywhere.

"Why do I have to wear this again?"

Ashlyn glanced at her. She wore a lovely lavender dress the Sorceress let her borrow. It complemented her skin tone and the train covered her tail. A fashionable purple hat concealed her horns and completed the ensemble.

"So everyone doesn't know you're a demon and tries to burn you at the stake like last time. Remember?"

"Oh. Right."

"Besides, I think you look very cute." She took Thalia's hand in hers and squeezed.

Thalia stopped squirming. "Really? Okay, maybe clothes aren't so bad. But I'd still much prefer to be naked. And would really prefer you be naked."

Ashlyn rolled her eyes. "After we help the Sorceress, I promise I'll get naked to your heart's content."

Thalia hugged her tightly. "And let me dominate every single inch of your super-sexy Half-Elf body?"

Ashlyn sighed. "Yes you little nymphomaniac, you can treat me like the biggest slut in the five lands."

Thalia smashed her lips against Ashlyn's. "You have no idea how much I adore you."

Ashlyn smiled. She was getting some idea. But right now they needed to focus on helping Cassandra.

The Sorceress wore a cream-colored dress that highlighted her skin tone nicely and accentuated her lovely curves. Ashlyn thought Kiosa was going to have a very hard time resisting such a beautiful creature.

Well, if she calmed down that is. Cassandra was wringing her hands and frantically scanning the crowd. Zirena, she had it bad for this Corvarean warrior.

Ashlyn put her hand on Cassandra's shoulder, squeezing it gently. "It's going to be okay. You're the most beautiful and powerful sorceress I've ever met. And we'll be with you the whole time."

Cassandra put her hand on top of Ashlyn's. "Thank you. You're very kind. I... I'm sorry I..."

"Made us be your little sluts?"

"Um, yes... it's just... I get..."

"Lonely and wanted companionship?"

Cassandra's eyes lit up in wonder. "Yes! How did you..."

Ashlyn clasped Cassandra's hands in both of hers. "I'm always traveling from one town to the next, fighting demons and monsters. I know what it's like to be lonely. I get that you want someone to share your life with."

She glanced over at Thalia, who was looking at her in wonder.

Cassandra launched herself against Ashlyn and hugged her fiercely. Ashlyn was surprised but happily returned the friendly embrace.

"Thank you Ashlyn! I... I don't deserve you being this nice to me. But I am very appreciative that you are."

"Oh don't worry about making me your sex toy. Thalia loves doing that and I have the feeling will be doing it to me every night from now on."

"You're damn right!" the succubus piped up, poking her head over Ashlyn's shoulder. "And Cassandra, you gave me some wicked ideas on how I can turn this little slut into an even bigger whore."

"Thalia!"

The demon wrapped her arms around Ashlyn's waist and pressed her firm tits into her back. "What? I'm sorry, I'm a succubus, what do you want me to call you?"

"My name would be nice."

Thalia spun Ashlyn around and pinched her cute cheeks. "Okay, Ashlyn, I think you are the most beautiful creature I've seen in this world and the one beyond and I really want you to be my sexy slut."

Ashlyn sighed. How was Thalia able to be so charming while still calling her a slut? But that was probably the sweetest compliment Ashlyn had ever received. And she knew Thalia was being sincere. Her demon hunter abilities allowed her to read Thalia much better than normal mortals could.

She threw her hands around Thalia's neck. "Okay, fine, I'll be your slut. But you better take me on a date."

Thalia kissed her. "Sure. Um, what's a date?"

Ashlyn sighed again. Oh goddess.

"It's what we're trying to get for Cassandra."

"Ohhh. The human ritual of talking and eating before the intense, kinky fucking happens."

"Right." Well, it was close enough.

"Okay, let's get this Sorceress a date!"

*****

They found Kiosa in a tavern named *The Cheeky Barbarian*. It was a hospitable establishment with plenty of laughter and tall tale swapping going on among the patrons.

They settled into a table in the corner. Cassandra's breath caught and Ashlyn and Thalia followed her gaze.

"That's her," she whispered like someone in a delirious state of love.

Kiosa sat at a table across the room, engrossed in a fairly large tome. Her light brown hair brushed her shoulders and her skin was extremely tanned. It was hard to tell since she was sitting down, but Ashlyn was positive she was over six feet tall. She wore brown leather pants and a cropped tunic of a similar color that covered her breasts but not much else.

What most struck Ashlyn was her physique. She didn't think she had ever seen such an impressive physical specimen before. Kiosa was all well-defined muscle. There probably wasn't an ounce of fat on her. Ashlyn could easily understand why Cassandra was fantasizing about Kiosa's powerful arms taking her and ravaging her soft and sensual body.

"Whoa," Thalia commented, obviously just as impressed. "Cassandra, that woman can do so many extremely naughty things to you."

The Sorceress blushed. Telling Ashlyn that's exactly what she was hoping for.

Ashlyn refocused on Kiosa. "Well, she likes books. That's cool."

"Oh yes, I love that about her. I also adore reading. And she's reading one of my all time favorites right now."

Ashlyn squinted. Her Elven heritage gave her better sight than most people but even she couldn't make out fine print from this far away.

"You can see that?"

"I can use my magic to enhance my senses."

"Neat trick. So what's she reading?"

"*The Priestess's Revenge* by Nare Nasha. It's the last book in the Demon Wars Trilogy."

Ashlyn knew of the author but hadn't gotten a chance to read her books. Her demon hunting duties made it difficult to have time to read all the books she wanted.

"Demon Wars?" Thalia exclaimed. "Oh sure, I bet the demons are the bad guys."

"Um, well, yes," Cassandra replied.

"Typical. You mortals always give us such a bad rap."

Ashlyn could have pointed out all the nasty things demons did, but instead she kissed Thalia on the cheek.

"Well, you're a very sweet demon."

Thalia gave her that mesmerizing smile. "Aw, Ashlyn. Hey wait, don't spread that around. It'll ruin my reputation."

Ashlyn chuckled. "Okay, it will be our little secret."

Cassandra, meanwhile, had her head resting in her hands, staring forlornly at Kiosa.

Ashlyn leaned toward her. "This is the perfect opportunity. You both love the same book series. Go talk to her about that."

"I... I can't."

"Cassandra, you've faced down powerful monsters and evil wizards before, right?"

Ashlyn didn't know that for sure, but she could easily tell from Cassandra's abilities that she had to be one of the most powerful people in the entire five lands. And they had only seen a tiny fraction of her power. So there was a good chance she had seen her share of adventures.

"Yes."

"And you defeated them right?"

"Yes."

"How?"

"Well, I was confident in my abilities. I knew my magic wouldn't fail me."

"Exactly! So go apply that confidence right now."

"But... but this is totally different. This has to do with love and feelings."

Ashlyn sighed. She was right. It was totally different. Why did love have to be so hard?

Thalia poked her head in. "You know this would be a lot simpler if you just followed my advice. Go over there, strip out of your dress, and ask her to bend you over the table and ravage your pussy."

Ashlyn did her classic eye roll, which she was perfecting in response to Thalia's many outrageous sexual suggestions.

Cassandra had a similar reaction. "Thalia! I am not doing that. Especially with all these people around."

"Why not? I can smell the exhibitionist waiting to let loose inside you."

"Thalia!"

Ashlyn grinned. Thalia loved pulling that trick on her too, revealing all her kinky fantasies. The thing is, the succubus was never wrong about this kind of thing.

"Well, your muscular love over there is also thinking strongly about very kinky sex right now."

Cassandra blushed, staring at Kiosa and moving her hands unconsciously to her inner thighs.

"Oh, she must be on Chapter 12. There's a, um, very elaborate and steamy love scene in that chapter."

"Now this book is sounding like it's worth reading," Thalia decreed.

"I think what Thalia is trying to say," Ashlyn translated. "Is that she's in a perfect frame of mind for you to go talk to her. Trust me Cassandra, no one who likes women would turn you away."

The Sorceress looked like she was working up her courage.

She stood up.

She took a deep breath.

And then she plopped back into the chair.

Ashlyn and Thalia both let out a breath they were holding. Damn, so close.

"I... I'm sorry. I just can't."

Now it was Ashlyn's turn to look determined. She realized she was going to have to be more proactive in helping Cassandra. She wasn't sure why she was so invested in this. Being made a sex toy was a weird way to meet someone, but she had kind of become friends with Cassandra. And she related to a lot of what the Sorceress was going through. She really wanted to help her find love.

She leapt to her feet. "Cassandra, get ready to step in at the right moment. You'll know what it is."

"Wait, what?"

Ashlyn moved around the table, her eyes trained on the powerful and sexy Corvarean.

"Were are you going?" Thalia asked.

"I'm going to pick a fight."

She strode across the tavern. This was probably one of her dumber ideas. But she had committed herself, so she was doing it.

She snatched a tankard of ale off a table, drawing shouts of ire from the patron it belonged to, and marched right up to Kiosa's table.

Where she promptly hurled the liquid into her face.

It soaked her, splattering across her hair and the pages of

the book.

Ashlyn cringed internally. She felt bad about the totally unwarranted attack. But if it got Kiosa and Cassandra together, it would be worth it.

"Hey Corvarean! You're in my seat."

Kiosa didn't move at first. After a few moments, she took a cloth attached to her belt and dabbed at her face.

Then she looked up at Ashlyn. "You got my book wet."

Oh right. It was probably her favorite book. Ashlyn hated damaging books, but this was for a good cause after all.

"I did you a favor. Nare Nasha is an orc's cock of a writer. She writes total trash romance."

Ashlyn was sure that wasn't true. Even if it was, she enjoyed a good steamy romance novel. But she figured it would really piss Kiosa off.

The Corvarean warrior rose to her full height. Ashlyn looked up. She was taller than the average human woman but Kiosa soared a good half-foot above her. And her muscles looked so much bigger close-up.

But what she wasn't able to notice from across the room was what was between the warrior's legs. Ashlyn noticed a large bulge between her hips. Wow, Kiosa obviously had one impressive Corvarean cock. Now Ashlyn just needed to convince her to use it on Cassandra.

"No one insults Nare Nasha."

Okay, yup, that did it. She was definitely really pissed off.

Ashlyn decided to strike first, flashing out with a punch to Kiosa's gut. The Corvarean barely budged, looking like the punch tickled her at best.

Ashlyn stared up at her. Oh, this was very bad.

She picked Ashlyn up like she weighed nothing and hurled her across the room.

Ashlyn crashed onto a table, upending it and all the drinks

on it. Patrons scattered, getting out of Kiosa's way and cheering her on. Like seemingly every tavern across the five lands, everyone always enjoyed seeing a good bar fight.

Before Kiosa could reach Ashlyn, Thalia leapt onto her back and began whacking her in the head. Thalia wearing a dress and being flung this way and that as Kiosa tried to dislodge her was rather amusing. But Ashlyn really appreciated her friend coming to her aid.

Kiosa rammed Thalia back into the wall, removing the nuisance that was hanging onto her. Then flipped her onto another table, destroying it. Ashlyn hoped the Sorceress was cool with picking up the bill for all the damage they were doing.

Ashlyn flew like lightning across the room and delivered a powerful leaping side kick to Kiosa's chest. She actually succeeded in knocking the warrior back into the wall. That seemed to surprise Kiosa but didn't really hurt her much.

Ashlyn picked up the back of a broken chair and swung it at Kiosa's face. The Corvarean blocked it with her forearm and the wood splintered across her powerful limb.

She punched Ashlyn so hard she knocked the breath out of her. Then grabbed her and hurled her so high she bounced off the ceiling and then crashed back to the floor.

Ashlyn groaned loudly. That hurt so much.

As Kiosa advanced on her, she caught something out of the corner of her eye snake around the warrior's ankles. It was Thalia's tail!

She tripped Kiosa and the Corvarean crashed into another table, breaking it in half. The owner of the tavern was going to be so pissed at them.

Ashlyn leapt to her feet, knowing this was her opportunity. She had been trying to avoid Kiosa's face, so she looked nice for Cassandra for when they hopefully hooked up. But she really didn't have much choice. There was no way she was going to have any luck hitting the rest of her body, which was pure muscle.

As Kiosa was getting to her knees, Ashlyn lashed out with a flurry of punches, backfists, and palm heels. Kiosa was a lot stronger than her, but she was faster. She finished the series of blows with a powerful knee to the face and blood spurted out of Kiosa's nose as she toppled to the floor.

Yes! Ashlyn knew it was only a momentary victory, but she felt proud she was actually able to knock down the seemingly unstoppable warrior. Though also guilty. She would have to apologize later for giving her a bloody nose.

She leapt into the air, soaring above Kiosa, looking to deliver a knockout blow.

But then the air crackled around her. Her body slowed, seemingly moving in slow motion. Kiosa stared at her wide-eyed, obviously mystified by what was happening.

"Leave her alone!" she heard Cassandra's voice boom on cue.

The air seemed to charge with electricity. And then a blast of lightning shot from Cassandra's hand and hit Ashlyn in mid-air.

She was thrown against the opposite wall, electricity coursing through her body. She knew Cassandra was using as little electrical charge as she could and that it would have been much more painful if she put her all behind it. But it still didn't feel good. It was like little static shocks were nipping at her all over her body.

Cassandra blasted Thalia with her other hand and the succubus was pinned next to Ashlyn.

The Sorceress magically removed rope from several adventurers' packs and sent them soaring toward Ashlyn and Thalia.

The lightning surrounding them dissipated, but they continued to float in mid-air as the ropes encircled them, tying their arms behind them and their legs together.

They fell to the floor next to each other, bound snugly.

Thalia managed to inch her body against Ashlyn's as the crowd erupted in cheers for Cassandra's amazing heroics.

"When you do things like that, I totally know why I'm falling in love with you."

Ashlyn's breath caught. Did Thalia just say she was in love with her?

She was trying to process that when Thalia kissed her and she immediately melted into her partner's loving lips.

She caught a glimpse of Cassandra kneeling beside Kiosa and holding her face gently in her hands, using her magic to heal the bruises on her face.

And then she knew only Thalia's lips and tongue. And they were the only thing that mattered to her. Even though she was bruised and bound, it had been totally worth it.

CHAPTER NINE

They went back to the Sorceress's house. Cassandra had informed the townsfolk that she would see to Ashlyn and Thalia's punishment. And she used her magic to take care of the damages.

So Ashlyn and Thalia pretended to be her prisoners and spent most of the walk back watching Kiosa and Cassandra being lovey-dovey. The powerful warrior carried Cassandra in her arms and they made out virtually the entire time.

Ashlyn smiled. Guess her plan had worked. She took Thalia's hand as they walked behind the new lovebirds.

Thalia curled her tail around Ashlyn's waist in that affectionate way of hers. "I want to make love to you so bad."

"Okay," Ashlyn replied agreeably. She wasn't going to try to have to be talked into it. She really liked Thalia and very much wanted to make love to her.

"While we watch those two fuck each other like wild Ashbats!"

"Thalia!"

"Oh c'mon, those two are so horny for each other it's going to be some of the kinkiest stuff you've ever seen. And I've seen a lot. And don't tell me you don't want to see Kiosa plow Cassandra's tight pussy."

Ashlyn couldn't tell her that. Well, if she did, she'd be lying. She was very eager to see the incredibly strong Corvarean totally dominate the sexy Sorceress.

"Okay fine, we can watch. But you better make me scream and cum as much as Kiosa makes Cassandra."

Thalia squeezed her tightly. "Challenge accepted sweetness!"

The fucking commenced almost immediately upon the four of them returning to the Sorceress's abode. Kiosa ripped Cassandra's dress off her in one fell swoop, while still kissing her, revealing that the Sorceress wasn't wearing any undergarments. That turned on the warrior even more. She quickly discarded her own clothing and bent Cassandra over the sturdy wooden table in the kitchen, pinning her arms behind her back with one hand.

She then proceeded to spank the Sorceress's hot ass really hard.

"Ah! Ahh! Ahhh!" Cassandra groaned in pleasurable pain. "Spank me harder!"

Ashlyn realized she and Thalia were squeezing each other very tightly, mesmerized by the ass spanking happening on the other side of the table.

Thalia looked at Ashlyn. "Clothes off. Now."

"Uh huh," Ashlyn readily agreed.

Thalia had her dress and hat off in an instant. Then helped peel Ashlyn's skintight leggings and top off her.

When they were both nice and naked, they looked back at their new comrades. Kiosa was now slapping the Sorceress's ass with her ridiculously huge, rock hard cock. Making Cassandra whimper in delight.

Both Ashlyn and Thalia's eyes went wide at seeing the monster between Kiosa's legs.

"That is one big cock," Thalia commented.

Ashlyn realized it must assuredly be a sight to behold if Thalia was impressed by it, considering all the shafts she must have seen in her succubus adventures.

Watching Cassandra and Kiosa go at it, added to her already burning desire for Thalia, was too much for Ashlyn. She needed to be fucked. Right now. And fucked hard.

"I need you to throw me on this table and do extremely wicked things to me."

"With pleasure," her demon friend said with glee.

She shoved Ashlyn face first onto the table, gave her a sultry spanking that jiggled Ashlyn's entire ass, and then hopped on top of her, straddling her, her sensual ass resting on Ashlyn's red cheeks.

As Ashlyn got ready for her already wet pussy to be plundered, she turned and saw Kiosa's cock monster slide into Cassandra's tiny pussy.

"Ohhhhhhhhh!" the Sorceress cried as her lips were penetrated.

Kiosa slid it in nice and slowly, letting Cassandra adjust to its girth and asking if she was okay.

Ashlyn was glad she had helped Cassandra get with a woman who was kind as well as being great at dominating her.

She was mesmerized by the slick shaft burrowing deeper and deeper into Cassandra's increasingly gorged pussy. Until her own pussy was pierced by Thalia's delicious tail.

"Uhh!" she groaned at the pleasant penetration.

Thalia laid flat against her, the succubus's massive, juicy tits rubbing against her smooth back. The demon reached underneath her and took two handfuls of Ashlyn's perky breasts and immediately got her nipples to stand rigidly at attention.

Thalia's tongue found her sensitive Half-Elf ear, running her snakelike tongue into all the most erogenous areas.

Ashlyn's voice rose in pitch as she was forced to make adorable sensual noises under Thalia's touch.

The succubus played with her tits masterfully, gave her the best ear fucking of her life, while banging her incredibly deep and hard with her flexible tail.

She opened her eyes to see how Cassandra was faring. Apparently really well.

Kiosa easily held the Sorceress's arms behind her with her one hand while the other hand firmly gripped one of Cassandra's ass cheeks and moved her thumb back and forth over her asshole. And, of course, while ramming her huge cock into her drenched pussy over and over again.

Cassandra was making some of the most erotic, submissive faces Ashlyn had ever seen. She wondered if she looked like that when Thalia dominated her. Probably.

Well, Cassandra was obviously having a great time if her screams were any evidence.

"Oh by the one true Goddess! Yes Kiosa! Fuck my tight pussy! Fuck it harder! Make me your Sorceress slut!"

That definitely motivated Thalia as Ashlyn felt the tail expand inside her and twist around so her entire pussy felt like it was beyond filled to capacity.

"Oh goddess!!"

"That's right," Thalia purred into her ear. "We can't let the Sorceress be the only slut here. Tell me what I want to hear."

Ashlyn knew Thalia loved it when she admitted how much of a whore she loved being for her. Right now, Ashlyn was more than happy to give her what she wanted. She was ready to turn her entire body over to Thalia's expert and loving care and let her to do whatever she wanted to her.

"Ohh Thalia! Please make me your fuck toy. Ravage my tight ass and pussy. Make me beg you to let me cum!"

Thalia probed deeply into her ear, making her squirm.

"That's what I like to hear you little whore."

She gave Ashlyn's nipples one last sultry tweak and then sat up, inserting her finger into Ashlyn's pussy next to her tail, and then sticking the coated finger into Ashlyn's ass.

"Ohhhh!" Ashlyn groaned loudly as her ass reflexively clenched around the demon's finger.

As she was fucked deliciously in both holes, she could tell Thalia was using her other hand to finger her demon pussy. She hoped Thalia would spray her succubus sauce all over her back, making her a good Half-Elf whore.

Kiosa was now ramming Cassandra so hard it was beyond what any mere mortal seemed capable of. The Sorceress was in such a delirium of pleasure she couldn't even get any moans out. But her face looked like she was having mind shattering orgasms. Like a lot of orgasms.

She finally let loose a primordial scream and her juices squirted out like a firehose around Kiosa's bulging cock. A cock which throbbed and let loose its own blast, pumping Cassandra full of delicious Corvarean cum.

The Sorceress squirmed as her pussy was filled and Kiosa grunted and yelled in pleasure above her.

A second later, Thalia twisted her finger and tail in Ashlyn's ass and pussy that made her cum instantly.

Her cries reverberated throughout the spacious house, like she was competing with Cassandra for who could be the louder slut. She was covering Thalia's tail in her juices and making a nice puddle on the table.

Thalia came right after her and Ashlyn felt a steady stream of the succubus's liquid coat her back. Thalia lifted her hips and made sure both of Ashlyn's ass cheeks were covered in her demon cum.

Then it was time for Kiosa to coat Cassandra. She pulled her cock out and released the rest of her seed all over the

Sorceress's back and ass, making her nice and sticky.

Thalia pulled Ashlyn up to a sitting position, so their legs were wrapped around each other. She ran her tail between Ashlyn's breasts and up to her mouth, flicking at her lips.

Ashlyn knew what the sneaky demon wanted her to do. She took the tail into her mouth and sucked her own juices off it.

Thalia softly ran her fingers through Ashlyn's hair. "That's right. Be a good little whore and suck it all off."

Ashlyn complied, feeling very naughty that she was doing whatever Thalia commanded.

"Now lick my cum off my fingers."

Thalia removed her tail and held up the fingers that were inserted deep into her demon pussy.

Ashlyn eagerly took them into her mouth and licked every ounce of Thalia's cum off them. She couldn't stop herself once she got a taste of the demon. It was like tasting pure heaven.

"Thalia, you... you taste so good," she told her lover breathlessly.

"Thanks sweetness. And don't worry. We're just getting started. I have a lot more plans to turn you into a total slut tonight."

Ashlyn shuddered. She couldn't wait to find out what those ways would be.

Next to them, Cassandra and Kiosa had already gotten started on Round 2. Kiosa had lifted Cassandra off the table and was spearing her on her once again very erect cock while standing. The Sorceress was hanging on for dear life as Kiosa forced her lover's hips up and down, making her take the entire huge shaft every time.

Ashlyn could tell Kiosa had complete control of Cassandra's body. She was so strong she was making Cassandra fuck her slippery shaft as fast and as hard as she dictated. Ashlyn thought back to a couple of days ago, when Corvan fucked her in the exact same position, his strong arms slamming her onto his beautiful cock as she let him control her pussy.

Oh Corvan. Dammit, what was she going to do about him? She really liked him. He was so sweet and kind. And she felt so comfortable around him and his mom. But she really liked Thalia too and was finding the succubus to be a surprisingly loyal and loving companion.

Ugh. This sucked. Well, this exact moment didn't suck. Because right then, Thalia laid her on her back on the table and straddled her face, obviously wanting Ashlyn to pleasure her pussy.

She happily did so, running her tongue up and down the succulent succubus lips and then plunging inside them.

Thalia gasped and threw her head back. Ashlyn always took pride in being able to get the sexy demon off.

Thalia's tail once again found Ashlyn's waiting pussy, and she tail fucked her wonderfully as Ashlyn went to town on the most delicious pussy in the five lands. Well, and probably in the underworld too.

She heard Cassandra beg Kiosa to make her the biggest magic slut ever. Which the sexy warrior was happy to do.

Their grunts and moans mixed with Ashlyn and Thalia's. It was a sweet, sexual symphony of different races and otherworldly beings.

Before long, Ashlyn got a nice cum facial from Thalia, and she hungrily lapped up every drop of the succubus's nectar.

She glanced over and saw Kiosa shoot more of her seed up into Cassandra's tender pussy. Then she lifted her lover off her and held the Sorceress in the air. Both Cassandra's cum and Kiosa's dripped out of her overworked cunt and formed a sultry puddle on the floor.

That sent Ashlyn over the edge, and she came hard from the way Thalia was working her tail inside her.

Cassandra collapsed into Kiosa's strong arms, while Thalia snuggled up to Ashlyn on the table, which Ashlyn had a feeling Cassandra might want to replace after how much they had been cumming all over it.

After her panting had mostly subsided, Cassandra waved her hands and golden trails of magic emanated from them and swirled all over her and Kiosa's body, focusing especially on Kiosa's cock and Cassandra's tits, pussy, and ass.

Ashlyn and Thalia watched in awe as the two lovers' bodies seized up and they both gasped. Kiosa's cock quivered rapidly and seemed to somehow get even bigger than the monstrosity it already was. Cassandra's nipples grew larger and harder than Ashlyn and Thalia had ever seen them. And her pussy seemed to throb with the need to be filled with the largest cock ever. Which Kiosa would fortunately be able to provide.

The magic threads floated over to Ashlyn and Thalia and infused themselves into their bodies, focusing the most on their private areas.

Ashlyn felt the effects immediately. Her nipples felt like they were on fire and got so hard and sensitive the gentlest brush of air caused her whole body to quiver. There was a raging inferno in her pussy. She needed every inch of it filled. Every inch of it fucked. Fucked beyond belief. Fucked until she came like a volcano. And then fucked more. Like all night long. She needed something in her pussy every minute of every hour of the day.

Holy fuck. This was some powerful magic. She had never felt this horny in her life. Not even close.

She saw the magic was affecting Thalia too. The succubus really didn't need any extra incentive to be super-horny and want to be constantly fucked. But Ashlyn could tell her demon lover was about to ravish her even more intensely than anything she had done before.

Thalia grabbed her and pulled her pussy against her own. The succubus's clit was extremely pronounced and she rubbed it against Ashlyn's. As soon as their pussies and clits touched, Ashlyn's entire body felt like it was having one huge orgasm.

With their legs crisscrossed, they pounded their dripping pussies against one another as hard as they could, both moaning uncontrollably.

"Ohh Thalia, I… I can't stop!"

"Me… me either. Ashlyn, your pussy… it's…"

"Oh goddess, harder! Harder!"

Their words dissolved into pants, moans, and cries of bliss as they pussy fucked each other and spread more and more of their juices all over each others' bodies.

Ashlyn threw her head back and saw Cassandra and Kiosa. They were just as frenzied in their lovemaking. Cassandra's perfect ass was slamming into the wall as Kiosa pounded her pussy like her dick had finally found its long lost home.

The warrior's naked body was a work of art, all taut muscles and tightness, wonderfully juxtaposed with Cassandra's softer, sensual curves.

"Oh Kiosa!" Cassandra cried out. "Please… please take me upstairs and make love to me all night long. I never want your cock to leave my pussy!"

"As you wish milady."

Kiosa took her in her arms and climbed the stairs, somehow spearing her up and down on her massive shaft the whole way to Cassandra's bedroom.

Ashlyn smiled. Kiosa was gallant, caring, and an epic lover. Cassandra really knew how to pick them.

She turned her attention back to Thalia and her wonderful,

perfect pussy. A pussy she couldn't get enough of.

After they squirted all over each other from their pussy grinding, they spend the rest of the night finding inventive ways to fuck each other.

They shoved various fruits and vegetables they found in the kitchen in each others' tight holes. They tied each other in the kinkiest, most submissive positions possible and gave each other orgasm after orgasm. Ashlyn rode Thalia's tail like a wild blazecat, coating the entirety of the sexy tendril in her cum.

They couldn't stop fucking. They couldn't go one instant without their bodies touching. They needed each other. They were consumed by each other. Their orgasms melded into one and overwhelmed them with pure pleasure.

*****

They woke up the next morning on the soft, lush rug in front of the fireplace, their bodies completely entangled.

Thalia's hair was in Ashlyn's face. She breathed in its lavender scent, sighing contentedly.

"Did... did that actually just happen?" she asked, wondering if it was just one huge sex dream.

"It sure did sweetness. That Sorceress is my kind of woman. Well, not as much as you are of course. No woman could be more amazing than you."

Ashlyn felt her heart flutter. She kissed Thalia lovingly. "When did you become such a charmer?"

"When I met you."

Her heart fluttered more. And she kissed Thalia deeper.

"Thalia, I..."

The cute demon put a finger to her lips. "Shh, just lay with me, okay?"

Ashlyn smiled at her. "Okay."

She nestled into Thalia's warmth and felt just how tender her muscles were. "I don't know if I can do much else with how sore I am."

"I know what you mean. My tail is throbbing."

"Oh, I'm sorry. I... I was kind of rough on it last night."

Thalia smooched her again. "Don't worry sweetness. I like it rough."

They lay together, completely content to listen to their lover's breathing and feel the cozy body next to them.

Ashlyn couldn't believe she had become this close to a demon. But she was very glad she had. And she knew she didn't want to lose Thalia. In fact, she would have been content to lay like this with her forever.

They were finally roused by Cassandra and Kiosa coming down the stairs. They joined the new lovers for breakfast, Cassandra giving the table a vigorous magical cleansing of all the succulent juices that had been spilled on it from the previous night.

They ate ravenously. They had all worked up quite an appetite from last night. Even though Thalia didn't need food, she happily stuffed her face, never one to turn down delicious sustenance. Ashlyn had let her sexually feed on her before the Sorceress and warrior had rejoined them, so she knew Thalia had been sated.

After the main eating was done, Cassandra sat sideways on Kiosa's lap. They fed each other fruit and looked very much in love.

"You two seem to be hitting it off," Ashlyn said with a grin, happy her new friend had found the love she wanted so badly.

"Oh yes," Cassandra said with a cute blush. "We have a lot in common. We spent the whole morning reading books to each other."

Kiosa brushed Cassandra's hair behind her ear. "Indeed. Cass is as intelligent as she is beautiful. But we didn't spend the entire morning reading my love."

Cassandra blushed more. Ashlyn knew exactly what other activity they had been up to.

So did Thalia. "Well that's a relief you got in some kinky fucking and didn't just read boring books the whole time."

Ashlyn shoved her. "Stop teasing them."

"Okay," the mischievous demon agreed all too readily. "I'd rather tease you anyway."

Ashlyn stuck her tongue out at her, but Thalia snatched it with her own tongue and pulled Ashlyn into a fierce kiss.

They heard an "Aww" from across the table.

"You two are so adorable together," Cassandra chirped.

"You really are," Kiosa echoed.

Thalia wrapped her arms around Ashlyn's neck and squeezed her tightly, obviously thrilled by their commentary.

"Well, so are you two," Ashlyn returned the compliment. "And Kiosa, I'm sorry I…"

The warrior held her hand up. "There's no need to apologize Ashlyn. Cass explained everything to me last night. If you hadn't acted, we might never have gotten together. For that, I am grateful. And might I add that you are a formidable warrior. I was very impressed by your fighting prowess."

"Oh," Ashlyn replied, a little surprised. That was high praise indeed coming from a Corvarean. "Um, thank you. You're ridiculously impressive yourself. I mean at fighting."

"And at fucking!" Thalia chimed in. "I can't believe how much of a total slut you made our sexy Sorceress here."

Ashlyn elbowed Thalia. Not that the succubus was wrong. It was just she needed to learn a little tact.

Cassandra blushed furiously, but Kiosa smiled.

"Oh you mean like this?" she said as she lifted Cassandra

off her lap, rotated her away from her, and slid her pussy onto her instantly erect cock.

"Oh Goddess!" Cassandra cried out in surprise.

Ashlyn and Thalia were just as surprised, their eyes going wide.

"Yup just like that!" Thalia responded, always happy when someone was getting fucked.

Cassandra squirmed on the huge shaft as she sunk deeper and deeper on it. "Kiosa, I…"

"Now now Cass. Remember you promised last night you would be a good little slut and be my sex toy today. Sex toys need big cocks inside them, right?"

"Uhhh, r… right."

Kiosa brushed her hair out of Cassandra's face again. "Don't worry lover. You can use your amazing magic to do kinky stuff to me later. But for today, you get to be my naughty slut."

She bounced Cassandra on her lap, making the Sorceress whimper from the gigantic shaft thrusting into her.

"Ohh yes! I want to be so naughty for you."

Ashlyn and Thalia looked at each other.

"Okay, I think that's our cue to leave," Ashlyn announced. Not that she wouldn't have enjoyed watching these two incredibly sexy women make love again, but she figured they should have some alone time to really get to know each other.

"Wait," the Sorceress commanded.

She touched Kiosa's cheek gently. "My love, I must talk to them for a moment. I promise I'll return to your wonderful cock as soon as I'm done."

"Of course Cass. Take your time."

Cassandra eased herself off Kiosa's monster and approached Ashlyn and Thalia, taking their hands in hers.

"Ashlyn, Thalia. I cannot thank you enough for what you

did for me. You are true friends and I will be forever in your debt. If you ever need anything, squeeze this and call my name."

She deposited two amethyst gems in their palms and infused them with magic. Then she hugged them both fiercely.

Ashlyn squeezed her shoulder and smiled at her while Thalia kissed her on the cheek.

"Oh, there is one thing I can do for you now," Cassandra told them. "Close your eyes and think of a place where you feel the most safe and content."

Ashlyn wasn't sure why they were doing this, but she played along. She trusted Cassandra.

"Take each other's hand."

Ashlyn reached out and found Thalia's soft palm. She clasped it tightly and pictured a place in her mind.

When she opened her eyes, she wasn't in Cassandra's house anymore. She was on a farmstead. A very familiar farmstead.

It was Corvan and Rima's house!

She felt a hand squeeze hers. She looked over and saw Thalia was still beside her.

"Huh? The hunky farmhand's house, right?"

"Um, yeah. His mom made me feel like part of the family so I thought of here. What... what did you think of?"

"I thought that I wanted to be wherever you were."

Ashlyn's heart melted. She pulled Thalia closer. "Thalia, I don't want you to think... I mean, what I'm trying to say is..."

Shadses, why was this so hard? She took a breath.

"I... I really like you. And just because I brought us here doesn't mean..."

Thalia put a finger to her lips again. "I know sweetness."

And then her sweet lips were on Ashlyn's. And Ashlyn knew everything would be okay.

Until the door opened.
And she saw Corvan and Rima there.
Watching her make out with Thalia. Totally naked.
Oh shit.

Thank you so much for reading this first collection of Demon Hunter Ashlyn stories! Look for more of Ashlyn's sensual fantasy adventures coming soon!

Sign up for my **E-Mail List** at RileyRoseErotica.com and get a **free eBook**!

Please Follow Me on my Amazon Page so you can be alerted to all of my new books and see all my current stories in publication.

Check Out My Other Fun and Sexy Books - Now Available on Amazon!

Laia Rios: Sex Raider Series
Laia Rios is the most amazing adventurer and relic hunter on the planet. When she gets word of a new clue to the legendary Lust Idol of the Amazons, she can't pass up the opportunity to find it. And all she'll have to do is pass through a temple filled with the most elaborate sex traps ever and submit her body to a bunch of Amazons with the most amazing bodies on the planet. Will Laia be able to withstand all the Amazons' physical and sexual tests? Find out if the Sex Raider is up for the challenge in this sexy and fun action/adventure erotic series!

Lust Hunters: Wicked Desire
Special Agent Jess Ballantine has to deal with her burning desire for her best friend Casey while trying to survive lustful zombies! It's hard to fight the undead when something is making Jess and Casey horny as hell. Can they fight their lust for each other and for the zombies? Will they find a cure before they turn into sex zombies themselves? It's a race against

desire in this action erotica!

The Mara and KATT Sex Chronicles
Mara Keoni is a sexy Navajo special agent of the Independent Justice Foundation. But she never expected to be paired with KATT, an incredibly advanced female AI inside a sports car. Not only is KATT very eager to help Mara on her missions, but she's also eager to pleasure Mara in every way possible with her many "enhancements." Will Mara succumb to her curiosity and find out exactly what KATT can do to her? Find out in Submitting to My Robot Car and Seduced by My Robot Car - Books 1 and 2 of The Mara and KATT Sex Chronicles!

Submitting to My Neighbor the Witch
Elena Cortez loves Halloween. So when her new sexy neighbor Cassia invites her to a Halloween party, she's super-stoked! Only problem: Elena thinks Cassia might be a witch. Like a real witch. Who's using her magic to make Elena have the most epic orgasms of her life! Will Elena be able to discover the truth about Cassia? Will she let herself become the ultimate witch slut? And will she let Cassia put her wand wherever she wants? Find out in this fun, Halloween-themed erotica!

Visit RileyRoseErotica.com to learn more about my books and the Decadent Fantasy Universe!

E-mail me at Riley@RileyRoseErotica.com. I would love to hear from you!

Check Out My Sexy/Geeky Social Media Links!

Facebook.com/RileyRoseErotica

@RileyRosErotica on Twitter

@RileyRoseErotica on Instagram

About the Author

Riley Rose loves writing fun and adventurous erotic fiction set in the action and fantasy genres, focusing on stories with heart, humor, and characters who keep losing their clothes. Riley is working on a shared universe of erotica, the Decadent Fantasy Universe, where characters from different series and stories will crossover with each other. Blending action, humor, and sexy shenanigans, Riley brings a unique blend of sweet and sexy stories featuring fun-loving characters, whose adventures you'll hopefully want to follow for a long time. Find out more at RileyRoseErotica.com.

Made in the USA
Middletown, DE
30 November 2021